"Do you think the person you saw could have been your brother?"

Emma shook her head. "No. I'd know my brother if I saw him. Wait, are you asking me that because you think I saw Austin and I was trying to hide it?"

Cole shrugged. "I had to ask," he said mildly.

"Well, now you have." She clamped her mouth shut.

She resumed walking toward the exit, tired and annoyed and angry and sore.

And *scared*. For her parents, especially her dad, who was now going to have to testify in open court against a stone-cold killer. And for her brother, who might have already been taken captive by the bad guys.

Chilled, Emma flicked up the collar on Cole's windbreaker. The clinic and its adjoining parking lot were on the edge of Bear Lake.

Bang!

They were almost at his truck when a gunshot cracked across the parking lot, immediately followed by two more shots.

Cole hollered, "Gun! Get down!"

One moment Emma was staring down at asphalt covered with rainwater...and the next moment, someone came up from behind and threw a blanket over her head, draggin

Jenna Night comes from a family of Southern-born natural storytellers. Her parents were avid readers and the house was always filled with books. No wonder she grew up wanting to tell her own stories. She's lived on both coasts but currently resides in the Inland Northwest, where she's astonished by the occasional glimpse of a moose, a herd of elk or a soaring eagle.

Books by Jenna Night

Love Inspired Suspense

Big Sky First Responders

Deadly Ranch Hideout
Witness Protection Ambush

Range River Bounty Hunters

Abduction in the Dark
Fugitive Ambush
Mistaken Twin Target
Fugitive in Hiding

Rock Solid Bounty Hunters

Fugitive Chase
Hostage Pursuit
Cold Case Manhunt

Visit the Author Profile page at LoveInspired.com for more titles.

Witness Protection Ambush

JENNA NIGHT

LOVE INSPIRED SUSPENSE
INSPIRATIONAL ROMANCE

LOVE INSPIRED® SUSPENSE
INSPIRATIONAL ROMANCE

Recycling programs
for this product may
not exist in your area.

ISBN-13: 978-1-335-98021-2

Witness Protection Ambush

Love Inspired
22 Adelaide St. West, 41st Floor
Toronto, Ontario M5H 4E3, Canada
www.LoveInspired.com

Printed in Lithuania

FSC

MIX
Paper | Supporting
responsible forestry
FSC® C021394
www.fsc.org

Therefore if any man be in Christ,
he is a new creature: old things are passed away;
behold, all things are become new.
—*2 Corinthians* 5:17

For my mom, Esther. Always an encourager.

ONE

"Single vehicle crash. Sedan struck a tree. I'll check with the occupants and see if there are any injuries."

Part-time EMT Emma Hayes was actually off duty as an emergency responder for the small mountain town of Cedar Lodge, Montana. She was on the way to her second job as a librarian when she came across the accident scene along a narrow road skirting the edge of Bear Lake. But she always kept her emergency radio with her in case she came across situations like this when someone needed her help. She gave the dispatcher the specifics on her location.

"Copy EMT-26" came the staticky reply over the radio. The town was in a narrow valley surrounded by jagged mountain peaks and radio reception wasn't always the best. "Standing by for your update."

There was more radio traffic after that, but Emma tuned it out for the moment as she pulled up closer and parked. Lakeside Drive was curvy as it edged along the waterfront on one side and a grassy, forested hill on the other. Emma had caught a glimpse of the dark green four-door a few moments earlier, but she'd had the impression that it was parked alongside the shoreline. At the very least, it hadn't had the front bumper pushed up against a big pine tree like it did now.

She grabbed the basic first aid bag that she kept in the car—she didn't carry the advanced equipment the paramedics had, but it was definitely better than nothing—and got out. She approached the car and yelled, "Hello! You okay in the car? Anybody hurt?"

The car made some ticking, settling noises as a result of the crash.

Lord, please let the person or persons in this car be okay. And if they need my help, please guide my actions.

The driver's-side door was open, likely knocked that way in the collision. Emma approached it, concerned when she didn't see the driver's head, and she prepared herself to see them slumped over the steering wheel, possibly unconscious. But when she looked into the vehicle, she didn't see a driver. She didn't see anybody.

The accident had happened just moments ago. She put a hand to the dented hood. It was still warm.

The crunch of a footstep on gravel pulled Emma's attention toward two men walking in her direction. Like her, they were on the lake side of the road and they'd apparently been hidden from view by the trees. The occupants of the crashed car, she assumed. They must have gone searching for help. This stretch of road didn't get much traffic in the late morning.

It seemed strange, though, that they'd gone in the direction they had. Because the main section of town—where they could have found people and businesses—was in the opposite direction.

But they had just been in a crash. Could be that they'd bumped their heads and they were addled.

With her determination to help undiminished, Emma sped up to close the gap between them. "Hey, what happened?" she called out. "Are you guys okay?"

"We're fine," one of them—a bald man with a beard—called out. "Must have been a problem with the brakes."

His companion, a tall and slender guy with a pony-tail, said nothing.

Both of them fixed their gaze on her in a way that caused her to slow her pace without consciously deciding to. And then she realized her mind had registered something. In the dappled light shining down through the branches of the trees alongside the road she saw sunlight glint off of an object. It was metallic and located just below Bald Man's right hand. The same kind of glimmer showed itself beneath Ponytail Man's right hand, too.

Guns.

Emma stopped. Her breath caught in her chest and her body tensed.

Eight years after her family was whisked out of Los Angeles and dropped into northern Montana, she'd believed they were safe. She'd imagined the threat was over.

Maybe this was unconnected to all of that. Maybe it was just some random robbery.

No, she knew better than that.

She thought of the car crashed into the tree. No occupants. *A staged accident.* Their witness protection handlers had told them stories of people who'd been captured and tricked by pursuers in the past. But those witnesses hadn't been securely hidden with solid cover stories and new identities. They'd all been people trying to evade the bad guys on their own. The point of the stories was to convince Emma's family to go into the protection plan.

"Emma Burke," Bald Man called out her old name. Well, same first name, old last name. Either way he confirmed what she'd just thought. He knew her true identity.

So what had happened? How had they found her? And

what about the rest of her family? Fear twisted her heart. Had they already captured her parents and her younger brother?

Her thoughts froze as Ponytail Man raised his gun and pointed it at her. "You're going to have to come with us."

Her heart thudded so hard that for a moment it was all she could hear. Her body began to shake. She was on the sharp edge of panic with no idea of what to do. Emergency responders should be on their way, but waiting and hoping they'd get here in time was not a great plan.

A loud growling sound caught her attention. Someone riding a personal watercraft on the lake jammed by with the throttle fully opened.

Emma realized the gunmen were also distracted by the loud noise.

Run! Now!

She let the bulky first aid kit drop to the ground and darted across the road and up into the forested grassy hill. Her emergency radio slipped through her fingers. The crack of a gunshot kept her from stopping to retrieve it.

She still didn't have a coherent plan, just a panicked impulse to survive and get to her family to warn them— if they hadn't already been discovered and snatched up by Royce Walker's criminal gang members.

She raced up the grass- and tree-covered hill, immediately feeling short of breath, as if her lungs were locking up. Some of it was triggered by panic and exertion, but there was no mistaking the tight, wheezing sensation of an asthma attack. And of course her inhaler was in her purse back in the car.

She forced herself to continue on. Trying not to leave a trail was hardly an option when it took all of her focus to keep moving and breathe. Finally, she slid behind a group of towering pines with thick trunks and a deep bed of dropped, dried needles at the base. Maybe she could bury herself underneath it. But first, she had to catch her breath.

Listening carefully, she dared hope that the pursuers were straight out of Los Angeles where the gang was centered and that they were helpless and unable to track anybody in the woods.

The sound of male voices along with footfalls in the wild grass and atop fallen pine cones confirmed that her hope was misplaced.

Where was everybody? Where was the cop who should have been on scene by now? Why were they taking so long? Even though she hadn't given the dispatcher an update, some kind of official response should have been activated.

With the next labored breath she realized that it hadn't been so long since she'd called in the crash. Just a few minutes. Of course all the emergency responders knew minutes could be critical, but you could only do so much. There were immutable laws of physics. There were other vehicles on the road and sometimes trains at railroad crossings. Even when you were responding to a call and desperately wished those things were not in your way, they were.

The tightness in her lungs eased a little. She didn't want to go farther up the hill because of the added exertion triggering her asthma, but heading that way made the most sense. It might not feel like it right now, but this was a relatively small hill. On the other side it dropped down into the edge of town where there were small farms and then farther on some streets with houses and shops. There had to be somebody in the vicinity who would help her. And maybe if she got to a populated area, that would be enough of a deterrent to make the gunmen back off.

Her body tensed with fear as the sounds of the pursuers grew louder. She pushed herself to her feet and continued up the hill.

She was gasping loudly now. She couldn't help it. Each step felt like her foot was chained to a block of cement. Sweat ran down to her brow and into her eyes. She told herself that she could rest when she was safe. Right now she had to keep moving.

She avoided the open areas on the hillside and kept to the shadows beneath the trees until she finally reached the top. She didn't hear anyone following her and she *had* to rest for a moment. Pressing her hand against a tree trunk to help her keep her balance, she took a moment to just breathe.

Bang!

A bullet tore through the tree trunk beside her hand.

Fresh waves of icy terror sent her diving to the ground and frantically trying to roll out of the way of gunfire. She tucked her body into a ball, desperately shrinking her profile so she wouldn't get hit as one of the thugs fired another shot.

After a few moments of quiet, she got back to her feet and continued down the hill on the other side to put some distance between herself and the attackers. But it was clear that continuing along in the same direction was no longer a good option.

New plan. Forging a different path, she'd head back the way she'd come. If she moved quietly enough, maybe the gunmen wouldn't realize she was doubling back to the road.

She'd just have to breathe the best she could while moving quickly enough to get to her car. Then she could drive away before the creeps noticed. She'd go directly to her parents' house to make sure they and her brother Austin were okay. Even better, she could grab her phone from the purse she'd left in the car and maybe even retrieve her emergency radio if she came across it and alert everyone in the county about the dangerous situation that was happening.

Doing her best to ignore the fear that nearly overwhelmed her and focus on a good outcome instead, Emma pushed herself to hike back downhill and toward the road.

Halfway there it was painfully obvious that her body was not receiving the benefits of optimal amounts of oxygen. Her head was pounding and her gait was stumbling and clumsy. But she kept going, telling herself that she was almost to the street and soon she would be safe.

She pushed through the edge of the forest where it met the road, grateful to see that she was very close to her car. It was only a few steps away. But she *had* to take a moment and at least partially catch her breath before she fell over. She was lightheaded and her vision was getting blurry. Her fight to save herself would all be for nothing if she passed out here.

She didn't hear the bad guys behind her, so she figured she could just take a couple of good breaths and then move on. Well, as good as they would be in the middle of an asthma attack.

Exhausted nearly to the point of collapse, she bent forward and braced her hands on her knees as she took first one breath and then another. Then it was time to get moving again.

But before she could straighten, she felt the tip of a gun barrel press against the back of her neck followed by the voice of Bald Man. "It was a mistake to stop. You should have kept running."

* * *

Paramedic Cole Webb knew something was *off* as soon as he arrived on-scene.

It had been years since he'd served in a combat zone as a Navy corpsman routinely heading out on patrol with a squad of Marines, but the old instincts and habitual vigilance had never completely left him. Not even back home in Cedar Lodge.

He brought his pickup truck to a stop on the side of the road and began cataloging what was in front of him while considering what could have triggered his unease. Emma Hayes's SUV was parked by the side of the road but there was no Emma in sight. That was concerning. Initially he'd thought she might be working with patients on the ground and she was hidden from view by her car, but now that he could take a closer look, it was obvious that wasn't the case. In fact, he didn't see anybody at all.

"Dispatch, this is Webb. I'm on-scene at the single car crash. No sign of EMT-26 or the driver of the other vehicle. I'm going to look around."

"Copy," the dispatcher replied. "I've been waiting to hear back from EMT-26. Update as soon as possible."

Cole had just completed a fifteen-hour shift as a paramedic with the Cedar Lodge Fire Department. He'd been scheduled to work twelve hours, but a multi-vehicle crash with major injuries on the highway west of town this morning meant he was working for as long as emergency services needed him.

He'd heard Emma's initial transmission regarding the single vehicle accident. With resources already stretched thin and no report of the immediate need for emergency medical response or police assistance, her call dropped to a lower priority. Not an ideal situation, but an emergency system could only do what they could do.

When his shift finally concluded, he'd let dispatch know he would check on Emma. This was his usual route around the eastern edge of the lake and over to the ranch where he lived with his grandfather, his cousin and her husband. Emma, he knew, would have been on her way to the tiny Meadowlark branch of the public library where she worked a half day on Mondays.

"Emma, I'm here at the accident scene," he said into the handheld emergency radio all the first responders carried even when off shift. Cedar Lodge was a beautiful town, but it was also fairly remote. People needed to look out for each other as much as possible.

He'd already reached Emma's car and as he glanced inside he heard a sound to his left, seeming to come from the side of the road. It sounded like a radio transmission. He looked over and spotted an emergency radio on the ground. The transmission he'd heard was his own voice. That had to be Emma's radio.

His initial concern shifted to a chill racing up his spine. Something was *very* wrong. He quickly turned his attention back to the inside of Emma's car, searching for signs of foul play. There was no visible blood, but her purse and phone were on the front seat. His pulse quickened as his heart kicked into overdrive. Emma would not have intentionally, willfully, left all these items behind.

He checked the other vehicle. Looked like minor damage at first, but enough of a dent on the front left fender to make the car not drivable. No skid marks on the road, which indicated the driver hadn't hit the brakes in an attempt to regain control of the car. Was this an intentional collision?

If there was some kind of criminal activity going on, why hadn't the driver of the crashed car taken Emma's vehicle to leave the scene? Was the driver aware that Emma worked for emergency services and that most of the cops in town would recognize her SUV? Anyone who took it would be quickly apprehended.

Cole keyed his radio and requested that dispatch roll a law enforcement unit to the crash site.

A familiar voice popped onto the radio almost immediately. "Dispatch, show Volker en route to Webb's location." It was Officer Kris Volker, a friend of Cole's since their school days and an excellent cop.

Cole took a breath and focused his thoughts. He glanced at the dirt and grass beside the crashed car and also beside Emma's SUV, looking for an extra set of tire tracks. If assailants had grabbed Emma for some reason and left their own car as well as Emma's SUV behind, wouldn't that imply that they had accomplices with another vehicle for the getaway?

But why would somebody grab Emma?

They'd worked a few shifts per month together for two years. She'd started as a volunteer with the fire department when she was twenty. At the time Cole had thought of her as a kid. Not only was she eight years younger than Cole, but she'd lived a quiet, predictable life in Cedar Lodge while Cole had been in combat and had spent time in places around the world far different from northern Montana.

But then he couldn't say he knew her life story. Of course they talked when they worked together, but they kept things professional. He knew she hoped to be a full-time librarian someday, but she could only get a part-time gig doing that for now. She'd told him she had to wait for someone with more seniority than her to quit or retire before she could get a full-time librarian job. Not exactly the kind of job that Cole could personally imagine sacrificing a lot of time waiting for an opportunity, but he had to admire Emma's determination.

A shadowy thought flickered across his mind. Maybe Emma had some other interest he knew nothing about and that interest had drawn her into a dangerous situation. Plenty of people had some aspect of their life they liked to keep hidden. Cole had seen evidence of that many times. Why should he be surprised if Emma turned out to be no different?

Cole's own father was not the man he'd pretended to be. He looked clean cut and fooled lots of people while he was actually a criminal lacking ethics or a conscience. His father's deception, revealed after his parents were married, might not have literally killed Cole's mom, but he was certain the stress of it had contributed to her poor health. She died when Cole was still in high school.

Enough.

Emma's personal life was not his business. Didn't matter if she was living some kind of secret life. Right now he needed to figure out what kind of trouble she was in and help her out of it.

Growing up on a ranch on the edge of the forest with his grandpa, Cole had obtained wilderness and survival skills long before he went into the military. Tracking was something he could do. If Emma was not taken from the scene by a vehicle, but by attackers who were on foot for some reason, then he had a pretty good chance of finding her.

Cole spotted trampled wild grass on the opposite side of the road a few yards away and took off in that direction. He had no idea what kind of situation he would be walking into and he had no weapon other than the short blade on the multi-use tool he carried on his belt. But he would find a way to improvise if he had to, because he couldn't just stand there and wait for Kris Volker to arrive in his squad car. He needed to see what kind of danger Emma was in right now.

Moving as quickly and quietly as possible while staying alert to his surroundings, Cole walked through the grass and up the hill into the forest. At least the path was unmistakable, with the grass just recently bruised. He guessed that he was following Emma plus one other person, possibly two. They were obviously heading up the hill and back toward town.

As an emergency responder he knew the streets and alleys and dirt roads of town and much of the countryside very well. He knew there was a small farm at the bottom of the hill on the other side. When he crested the hill he saw Emma walking with a man on each side of her. One guy with a long ponytail held her arm and kept yanking her forward as she stumbled. The other guy, a bald man, was yelling into a phone, but it wasn't clear what he was saying. Each man was carrying a gun in his free hand. They seemed to be headed for a dilapidated storage shed at the edge of the woods.

Cole didn't want to think about why they were headed there. To kill Emma and conceal her body? To hide themselves for a while because they knew someone was obviously going to be checking out the crashed car and Emma's SUV beside the road? The possibilities popping into his head were terrible, and he could not let any of them happen. Armed suspects with a hostage in a building was not a situation anyone wanted to deal with.

The small farm at the base of the hill looked quiet. If Cole could get someone to come outside, maybe that would redirect the thugs away from any of the outbuildings and back into the forest. Then Cole would have a better chance of keeping Emma from harm.

Skirting the edge of the woods and grateful the bad guys weren't bothering to look behind them, Cole picked up a rock and threw it at a farmhouse window. Glass shattered. Dogs inside the house started barking. As Cole had hoped, the attackers immediately changed direction and dragged Emma back into the cover of the woods.

Cole's phone buzzed. It was his cop friend, Kris Volker. "I'm on-scene, where are you?"

Cole gave a quick description of where he was, the direction he was going and what he'd seen.

"On my way," Volker said before disconnecting.

Cole couldn't let up in his chase. Volker was fast in an emergency, but in this instance he might not be fast enough. Fortunately, the assailants still weren't bothering to look behind them. They appeared to be on a panicked run to get deeper into the forest. Cole would use that to his advantage. He followed them into the shadowy woods and moved up closer on them.

Emma kept stumbling and the thugs were getting impatient. The one who had hold of her jerked hard on her arm and Cole was afraid the man would lose his cool and shoot her. When Emma finally tripped and fell, Cole grabbed the opportunity to jump on the back of the man with the ponytail who'd been hanging on to her. Yanking on the startled gunman's arm, he wrested the weapon away from him.

On the forest floor where she'd fallen, Emma turned to Cole, an expression of shock on her face.

Ponytail man scrambled into position to take a swing at Cole, but then the criminal saw Cole pointing his own gun at him and he froze.

The bald guy had already vanished into the forest. Cole hated to see the thug get away, but Cole wasn't a cop. He was a medic. And there was no missing the fact that Emma was having trouble breathing. He could hear her wheezing. She hadn't even said anything yet. Probably because she couldn't catch her breath. Cole knew she had asthma and he was concerned for her.

Ponytail guy, now without his gun, put his hands up. Then he slowly backed away. "See you later, Emma Burke," he said before disappearing into the dark forest.

"Cole." Emma sounded breathless when she said his name.

Mindful to keep an eye on their surroundings in case the criminals snuck back, Cole radioed Volker with the specifics on where they were and the current situation.

"Almost there," Volker replied.

Having done all he could, Cole squatted down beside Emma. "Take a minute to rest and try to catch your breath." Without even thinking about it he was already counting her respirations, which were too fast. He reached for her wrist to take her pulse and she burst into tears, moving her hand so that she was gripping him so tightly his hand went numb.

"I thought they were going to kill me," she said, gasping and crying as she tried to speak.

Against his better judgment, violating his own rule to keep things completely professional with all of his co-workers, Cole moved closer and wrapped his arms around her until she was clinging to him, her tears soaking his shirt. He could feel her heart racing as she was pressed against him. The paramedic side of him couldn't help confirming that it was beating way too fast. But the compassionate human side of him felt the stirrings of a protective tenderness that wasn't exactly part of his job description. Though normally a decisive man, for a second he wasn't certain what to do about that.

Finally, she released her grip on him and drew back. She was breathing a little easier but still wheezing. Tear tracks ran through the dust on her face.

"What happened?" Cole asked. "Who were those men? Where were they taking you? And why?"

She closed her eyes for a long moment, apparently steadying herself. And when she opened them again, she focused her gaze on his shoulder instead of his face before saying, "I don't know who they were or what they wanted."

She was lying. And he wanted to know why. In fact, there was a lot about Emma Hayes he wanted to know right now. He couldn't help being curious about the woman he'd thought he knew after working with her for two years. Whatever the situation was that she'd gotten herself into, he felt responsible for her safety. Maybe she'd made some bad decision somewhere along the line. Lots of people did. His own mother had made a bad decision in choosing his father. That hadn't made her a bad person.

Officer Kris Volker pushed his way through the pine trees and stepped up with his gun drawn and his gaze shifting as he surveyed the scene.

"I'm a little concerned they'll try to jump us as we make our way out of here," Cole said.

"I've got four more cops just a little bit behind me," Volker said.

Of course. Cops and medics oftentimes used cell

phones because anyone could listen in on a radio transmission. Just because Cole hadn't heard Volker call for backup didn't mean he hadn't done it.

When the other officers arrived to make sure everybody got out of the forest without any further trouble, Cole helped Emma to her feet. "I'm assuming your asthma inhaler is in your purse back in your car rather than in your pocket."

She nodded.

"Are there any officers still at the crash scene who could bring Emma's asthma inhaler?" Cole asked.

Volker shook his head. "I brought them all with me. I thought the perps might still be lurking nearby and we could catch them and bring them in." He glanced around. "Doesn't look like it."

Breaking another one of his rules regarding coworker professionalism, because apparently this was the day for it, Cole swept Emma up in his arms intending to carry her back to her car. It would be faster than having an officer go fetch her inhaler.

"Are you all right with my doing this?" he asked. "I don't think a hike would be good for you right now."

Wide-eyed, Emma nodded, her cheeks red with exertion or embarrassment, Cole wasn't sure which. "Yes, I'm okay with it. Thank you."

Relieved that she was alive and safe for now, Cole started walking back toward the road with Volker and the other cops accompanying them.

Emma *Burke*, the thug had called her.

It was Emma's choice how she lived her life, and maybe there were some details she kept hidden. Didn't matter what Cole thought about that. His immediate concern was for the safety of a coworker who was capable, diligent and kind. He worked as a first responder because he cared about the safety of the people in his town. He had some added skills thanks to his military service that could keep Emma safe until the cops got the bad guys. Cole would stay by her side as much as possible until this dangerous situation was stabilized.

Whatever her real name, whatever her true story, Cole had no doubt Emma was in serious danger. Whoever wanted her kidnapped no doubt *still* wanted her kidnapped. They would try again.

TWO

"Thanks," Emma said to Cole as he set her on her feet on the edge of the road after they exited the forest. She nodded her appreciation to a cop who'd already gotten her purse out of her car and brought it to her. She took a dose of the medicine that quickly eased her breathing.

She took a couple of deep breaths, wincing slightly at the sharp pain at her collarbone where she must have injured it when she fell. Then she turned to Cole with an awkward smile. "Now that I'm feeling better, let me properly thank you for checking on me and for dealing with those thugs."

His appearance from out of nowhere and attack on the man who'd been clutching and controlling Emma had been especially impressive. She'd known Cole was a military veteran with combat experience, but still, seeing a calm man she'd worked with on a regular basis leap into life-or-death action like that was something else.

"And thank you for carrying me while I was having trouble breathing," she added awkwardly. Suddenly she couldn't act normal around Cole.

She avoided eye contact with him because it was overwhelming having her work buddy rescue her so dramatically and then hold her so closely.

Okay, yeah, *she* was the one to grab him and hold him close for a moment or two right after he rescued her. And in the midst of that she'd felt something that she hadn't expected. Appreciation, but also something else. Something that had significantly changed her reaction to him. An unexpected attraction, actually.

"Happy to help," Cole said in that confident, easygoing manner that he always had. "Glad you're okay."

No doubt her cheeks were red with embarrassment when she finally glanced at him. He looked cool and collected as ever.

"Can you walk to your car?"

Emma nodded. "Sure. I'm perfectly fine now."

They walked side by side. Emma noted that the much taller Cole shortened his stride to match hers. Something he normally didn't do when they were working together.

The cop who'd brought her inhaler had left to rejoin the other officers. Volker had law enforcement on scene doing a quick search of the nearby streets looking for the kidnappers and conducting an interview with the residents of the farmhouse to see if they had any useful information.

A rookie officer Emma had seen on calls a couple of times stayed nearby and was checking out the crashed car as Emma and Cole approached.

"Have you gotten any information that could help identify the assailants from the vehicle registration?" Cole called out to the rookie.

The young cop shook his head. "The vehicle is on the stolen car hot sheet. Reported missing last night at the end of the owner's workday down in Baylor."

"Any chance the kidnappers' prints could be lifted?"

The cop shrugged. "Chief's sending a wrecker to tow it to the police garage so Tammy and her team can go over it."

These criminals are pros, Emma thought grimly. *Tammy won't find anything helpful.*

"What do you know about those men?" Cole turned to Emma. "Why'd they grab you? Where were they taking you?" It was the second time he'd asked her.

"I don't know."

"But the one guy knew your name."

Emma hated lying to Cole. He'd been a good work friend for years and just now he'd gone way beyond anything she could have imagined or expected in helping her. He could have gotten *killed* jumping on the gunman. But in a way, she'd been lying to him from the moment she'd first met him. She'd withheld the full truth of who she was because, for the sake of her family's safety, she had to.

Drawing on the determination and focus she'd had to use so many times after her life had taken the strange turns that had brought her and her family to Cedar Lodge, she lifted her chin to look directly into the blue eyes of the medic. "That guy had me confused with someone else. Didn't you notice that he used the wrong last name?"

The expression in Cole's eyes sharpened. Not like he was angry, but as if he didn't believe what she'd told him and he wasn't going to just let this go.

At the moment Emma was less concerned with his drive for the truth and more concerned about her mom and dad and Austin. She took a deep breath, felt that sharp pain at her collarbone again and reached up to it. Touching it only made it hurt worse and she sucked in her breath.

"Get in my truck and I'll take you to get that x-rayed," Cole said.

"Later. Right now I'm tired and I need time to rest."

He didn't look happy, but he gave her a curt nod of acknowledgment.

She turned away from him and sat down in the driver's seat of her car where she could grab her phone. She tapped the listing for her mom's number and the call rolled to voicemail. She took a deep breath and tried not to panic over the unanswered phone call. Maybe Mom had just gone to the store for something. Her mother didn't like to talk on the phone when she was driving, not even with a hands-free device.

Even as Emma told herself that semi-comforting story, she was pretty sure it wasn't true. Dread and fear settled heavy in her gut as she tried her dad's number and got his voicemail, too. And then she tried her younger brother, Austin. He didn't answer, either.

All the while, Cole lingered by her open car door.

"Did you actually see those men crash into the tree?" he asked her. "Did you see what caused them to swerve?"

"I didn't see the crash." Emma wasn't paying much attention to him. What if the bad guys had gotten to her parents and Austin? Fear for her family clawed its way up into her throat, feeling as if it might choke her. *Please, Lord, protect them.* She coughed and cleared her throat and began trying to call the numbers again, wishing for at least the thousandth time in her life that she had a *normal* family. If they didn't have this huge secret that must be kept she could call 9-1-1 and request that a cop make the drive to their house and conduct a welfare check. But doing that would lead to too many questions. And obviously, if they were a *normal* family, they wouldn't be in this situation.

While tapping her phone and then listening to her mother's voicemail response, Emma was vaguely aware of Officer Volker's voice coming through on Cole's radio. She was fairly sure one of the responders on scene would have found her own dropped radio by now and would get it back to her. Right now that was the least of her worries.

"I'm on my way back," Volker said through the radio. "Let Emma know I want to talk to her."

I'll talk to you for as long as you want after I know my family's safe.

Emma's hands shook with fear and adrenaline spiked in her system again as she imagined her parents and brother not answering her calls because the worst had happened.

Volker stepped out from the forest a few yards down the road and Cole walked in his direction.

Growing frantic with fear, Emma pulled her car door shut and turned on the engine. The cops didn't need her to stay on-scene. There was nothing here for her to do. Perhaps her mom and dad and Austin weren't answering their phones for some totally innocuous reason. Maybe they were all outside doing yardwork or washing their cars, completely unaware of the danger.

Maybe they weren't answering because they were gravely injured. But if she got to them in time they could be saved. For a split second she thought of asking Cole to come with her, but he was a by-the-book kind of guy and she didn't have time to argue. If she got to the house and her family needed help, Cole would be the first person she would call.

Already, he and Volker were looking in her direction, a questioning expression on both of their faces.

Emma lifted her fingertips to give a slight wave of acknowledgment before turning the steering wheel and hitting the gas so that she was headed back toward town and her parents' house.

She didn't have far to go. After skirting the edge of the lake for a couple of miles she hit town and made the turn into a hilly residential neighborhood with moderate-sized homes on acre-sized lots. She braked at a stop sign and noticed a cop car in the distance behind her. Possibly Officer Volker and Cole alongside him. The whole secret life her family lived was about to get blown apart. There was no getting around it now. Even a town cop and a paramedic knowing their true identities would compromise everything.

She threw aside that worry. The fact that the thugs had been able to find her proved that her family wasn't secure anymore, anyway. She should have already thought of that.

She pulled up the curving driveway to her parents' house, slammed the car into Park and leaped out.

The front door was partially open and there was a footprint on it, like maybe someone had kicked it open.

Emma knew she should be careful, but she couldn't make herself slow down as she pushed the door the rest of the way open and stepped across the threshold.

"Mom!"

No one answered.

A few steps farther and a turn to the right took her to the kitchen. The coffeepot was half full and still warm to the touch. There were a couple of dishes and some utensils in the sink ready for someone to rinse them and put them in the dishwasher. Her mom was a bit of a neat freak, and it wasn't like her to leave things that way if she was going out somewhere.

"Dad!" Again, no response.

Sick with fear, Emma opened the door to the garage. Both of her parents' cars were in there.

"Austin!" Now that her brother was eighteen and out of high school, he'd started to build somewhat of an independent life for himself. Officially, he lived at the house with his parents. In reality, he stayed with a couple of buddies from school who'd gotten an apartment together. Austin might not have even been in the house today.

Walking into the living room, Emma looked through the window at her dad's prized garden in the backyard. It was a beautiful combination of ordered flowers and rustic wilderness, with the back of the property opening up to forest. She strode toward the slider window. When it was nice out, her parents loved to sit on the patio and sip coffee and talk or get some work done on their laptops. Both of her parents worked from home.

Her heart sank when she saw the empty chairs at the table beneath a cheerful, floral umbrella.

Something moved at the edge of the yard.

The flash of motion and color wasn't a bird or an animal. It was too big. What she saw was less a clear image and more scraps of color that she put together in her mind to try and make sense of it.

Was it a man, maybe? In a red and black jersey?

Neither of the men who'd kidnapped her had been dressed that way.

She threw open the slider door—noting that it was unlocked—and started to step outside and yell at whoever it was. But at the last moment, she realized that probably wasn't a good idea. The person might be armed, like the thugs who'd grabbed her had been.

She stepped back into the living room, closing the door, and grimly told herself that she had to search the rest of the house even if she was afraid of what she might find.

"Hey, Emma. What's going on?"

Emma turned at the sound of Cole's voice. Volker was beside him, and both men looked very concerned.

"My parents—" She got only those two words out before she choked up and started to cry. "We need to search the rest of the house for them and my brother," she eventually added. It took a huge amount of effort to force out the words between racking sobs. The wave of emotion she'd fought to keep in check since today's horrible ordeals had begun was now crashing over her and there was nothing she could do about it.

To their credit, neither man questioned her. Instead, they walked down the hallway toward the bedrooms and family room while Emma waited and prayed and wiped the tears from her eyes.

"Nobody back here," Cole called out a few moments later.

He reappeared in the living room with Volker who said, "Let's check the garage."

"Their cars are here," Emma told them.

Volker nodded. "We'll go have a closer look."

They weren't gone long. "Nobody out there," Volker reported when they came back.

Cole walked over and stood in front of Emma. "Tell us what's going on."

What should she say? How much information might help her family if they were in danger? And how much would make things much worse?

"We need to find my family," Emma said after a significant pause. "That's what's important."

Cole gazed at the sable-haired woman who looked defiantly at him through coffee-colored eyes. "If we're going to look for them we need an idea of where to start."

She shifted her attention to Volker. "You can put out an alert for them, right? A be-on-the-lookout or something?"

"I can. But the search would be most efficient if you gave me all the pertinent information you have. Context for whatever is happening right now would be helpful."

Emma looked around the room, crossing and uncrossing her arms, then brushing her bangs back from her eyes.

Cole had seen her work under pressure during medical emergencies she'd responded to as an EMT. He'd been impressed by how calm and collected she was in the midst of chaos and people yelling or screaming. She'd been cool when he'd needed her to assist with life-or-death emergency procedures. He realized having her own family in danger made the situation different, but her angsty gestures still seemed out of character.

Then again, driving away from a crime scene before getting cleared by the cop in charge was out of character, too, even if it wasn't illegal. She knew the routine. Cole had been with her treating injured people at crime scenes on numerous occasions. Generally everyone hung around until they'd given a report of what they'd experienced or witnessed.

A transmission came through Volker's radio reporting that the wrecker had arrived to tow away the kidnappers' car and the scene was now officially cleared.

"Copy," Volker replied at the end of the update.

By now Emma had walked to the slider window where she stood rubbing her hands up and down her arms as if she were cold. While it was warm and sunny right now, Cole could see rainclouds closing in on the jagged mountain peaks in the distance.

"Someone was in the backyard when I first got here," Emma said as she turned around.

"Who?" Cole asked. He wasn't the official investigator here—clearly Kris Volker was—but Cole couldn't help butting in. As a military medic in a combat zone, he'd gotten dragged into situations that involved kidnapping and stalking and ambushes and all sorts of other crimes. He'd learned things beyond medical treatments that he could use here. In this case with Emma, he was determined to get more information.

He admittedly felt protective toward her, too. She was a smart, competent woman, but she was no street brawler. And since those thugs were willing to attack her once, it seemed a reasonable possibility that they'd do it again. Cole wasn't about to step out of the way and make it easier for them.

"I don't know who I saw at the edge of the garden," she said, glancing at Cole to answer his question and then averting her gaze.

What was she hiding? "Okay, who would you *guess* it was?" he asked.

She shook her head. "I don't have a specific idea. But I'd say it was an adult man. He moved fast so I'd say he must have been youngish. And he was wearing a red and black jersey." She shrugged. "That's all I can tell you."

Volker had been listening and he walked over to open the slider door and stepped outside. Cole went with him, while Emma stood at the doorway but remained inside the house. A wise choice, since someone could be out there waiting to take a shot at her. They took a quick look around, but didn't see anything significant. Nobody hiding. No sign anyone had spent a significant time hunkered down out there watching the house.

Emma had tears in her eyes when they walked back inside. "My family and I have been in a witness protection program for eight years," she said so quietly Cole barely heard her. It seemed like a struggle for her to say the words. "We were living under false identities. We kept the same first names but were given a new last name." She fixed her gaze on Cole. "That kidnapper in the woods who said he'd see me again before he ran away, he knew my real last name."

Witness protection? Living under a false identity? Cole felt like he'd had the wind knocked out of him. What else did he think he knew about her that wasn't true? And what else might she be keeping hidden?

"Apparently the people we've been hiding from have finally found us," she added, her voice breaking.

"Do you have a case handler you can contact?" Volker asked.

Emma startled. "Yes, I do. I don't know why I didn't think of calling him."

Because you were just abducted and nearly killed, Cole thought. She had to be traumatized and not thinking clearly, whether she was aware of it or not.

She stared at her phone for a minute. "I can't think of the name it's stored under," she said with a strained, nervous laugh. But after a moment she appeared to remember and tapped the screen, turning the phone on Speaker so that Cole and Volker could hear.

"Baker and Company," a female voice answered pleasantly.

Cole was surprised at first, but then realized it would hardly make sense for a secretive agency to answer a phone call by clearly identifying themselves.

"I need to talk to Cliff Martel," Emma said. "It's an emergency."

"I'll have him return your call." The woman spoke in the same, unemotional tone.

"I can't wait," Emma said, her voice growing louder. "My family could be in danger."

"I'm relaying the message right now," the woman answered. And then she disconnected.

For a moment Emma just stared at her phone, looking stunned.

"Did you have a safe place planned for your family to meet up in case your security is breached?" Volker asked.

Emma shook her head. "No. I was fifteen and my brother was ten when this started. My parents planned on us being together nearly all the time and assumed we'd be together if there was trouble. Since Austin and I are now both adults, security is focused mainly on our parents, not us." She shrugged. "Guess we're kind of on our own."

"Why would somebody come after you now?" Cole asked. "You said it's been eight years."

"I don't know." She shook her head. Then she took a deep breath and slowly blew it out, her eyes tearing up again. "Why did they want to drag me into the forest? Why didn't they kill me when they had the chance?" A tear rolled down her cheek and she wiped it away. "I thought they were going to," she added in a near-whisper.

"They might have grabbed you so they could use you as bait to draw out your parents," Cole said. Emma turned to him with a horrified expression and he winced inwardly. Volker was already nodding in agreement that it was a logical consideration.

"But it looks as if the bad guys already showed up here," Emma gestured toward the front of the house. "It looks like somebody kicked open the front door. If they'd already found my parents, why come after me?"

"By threatening to harm you, they could get your parents to do or say just about anything they wanted them to."

Even after learning the truth about Emma and her family being in witness protection, Cole still had no real idea what was going on. That was just one part of the story, and he was still trying to help Emma piece things together. "I'd guess having to chase after you in the woods wasn't in their plans," he said. "They probably somehow learned your work schedule, waited to stage the crash and knew as an EMT you would stop to help and then they could grab you. I imagine they thought you would be an easy target." Cole couldn't help smiling slightly at the reminder of what a *not*-so-easy target she had turned out to be.

She'd managed to evade the attackers until she could get help. Even with an asthma attack making things so much worse. She'd done everything she could and hadn't given up hope.

"The fender on their own car was dented too badly for them to drive away. In a small town like this, EMTs and cops obviously cross paths a lot and know each other. They probably figured if they'd taken your car for a getaway, they would have been found immediately."

Emma nodded, took a deep breath, and then tried to place calls to each of her parents and her brother again.

The sorrow on her face as each of the calls rolled to voicemail made Cole's heart ache in sympathy. Actively responding to an emergency medical call required a certain amount of emotional detachment. He could turn off his feelings while fighting to save a life, but trying to deny his emotions for very long led to some bad repercussions. He'd learned that lesson after his mom died when he was a teenager and he'd tried to avoid grieving her passing, and again after he left the Navy and initially tried to fit back into civilian life by living as if his traumatic memories could be ignored. At some point he'd accepted that

dealing with his emotions and even being a little bit tenderhearted wasn't the worst thing in the world. Not that
he went out of his way to let anybody know about the
tenderhearted part.

"I need both of you to go to the station with me so I
can get your official statements," Volker said.

"First I'll need you to give us a ride back to my truck,"
Cole said. Then he turned to Emma. "We should stop by
the ER and get your collarbone x-rayed before we go to
the police station."

"A walk-in urgent care place will be fine. It doesn't
hurt that bad."

She'd need to wear a sling for a few days or weeks if
her collarbone was indeed fractured. That would mean
she wouldn't be able to work any of her EMT shifts for a
while, but that would likely be the least of her concerns
right now. Finding her family and keeping herself from
getting attacked again were obviously more urgent pri-
orities.

"After we're finished at the police station, I'll go with
you to your apartment to make sure everything's okay."
Cole had never been to her home, but he remembered her
mentioning an apartment.

"Someone could be waiting for me there," Emma said
slowly, an expression of fear appearing in her eyes. "I
hadn't even thought of that."

"I'm sure everything there will be fine," Cole quickly
added, which was a polite lie. He wouldn't actually be
sure until he saw for himself that no one was lurking inside her apartment or nearby.

Emma glanced around the living room. "Hopefully I'll
hear back from my parents and my brother or the witness
protection handler soon. If not, I think instead of going

to my apartment I'd rather come back here. Maybe their situation isn't as dire as I think. Maybe they'll come back home."

Wishful thinking. He hated to take that away from her, but he felt like he had to. "I think staying here would be a very bad idea."

"Agreed," Volker added. He'd been standing near a window looking out at the street in front of the house. Now he took a step closer to the glass and pushed aside the edge of a sheer curtain. "Who's this?"

Emma took a look out the window.

A maroon sedan was coming up the driveway at a pretty good clip.

"I don't know who it is," Emma said. "I've never seen that car before."

THREE

"It has the look of an unmarked police vehicle," Volker said, remaining at the window. "But let's not take any chances." He gestured at Emma to take a step back into the room, away from the glass.

Cole moved closer to her, his nerves on edge and his focus shifting from the window to the front door and back again as he prepared to move fast if he had to. Emma had already been through so much today, but sometimes the fight had to continue even when you felt like you had no strength left.

"You should get behind me," he said to her quietly, but Emma's attention was fixed on the window and then the front door and she didn't seem to hear him. The vehicle came to a halt and a man got out and walked toward the front porch.

Cole and Kris Volker had been friends since they'd played sports together as young kids. The intuition they'd developed over the years to work together came into play now as they wordlessly coordinated their movements. Kris headed for the door and Cole followed him, placing himself between Emma and potential danger.

With his hand hovering near the pistol in his holster,

Volker pulled open the front door before the visitor had a chance to knock.

Cole recognized the plainclothes law enforcement officer standing there, though he couldn't immediately recall where he knew him from. The middle-aged man had salt-and-pepper hair and was dressed in jeans, a dress shirt and a sports coat. He pulled aside the coat to display the sheriff's deputy badge clipped to his belt.

"Newman," Volker said. "What are you doing here?"

"Probably the same thing as you. Checking up on Emma Hayes. I understand she drove here from the crime scene."

Volker opened the door wider and stepped aside to let the man in, then closed the door behind him. "This is Sergeant Rob Newman. He works for the sheriff's department. He normally works out of the substation at the far western end of the county."

Cole now realized that he'd worked a shooting scene with Newman a little over a year ago. The sergeant had recently joined the department after moving up from California.

"I don't know you," Emma said, suspicion darkening her tone.

"I'm here on behalf of Cliff Martel."

Her witness security contact.

"My parents are missing. Is Martel coming to help find them?"

"Actually, he's already been here and gone. He and his team moved your parents out of here to keep them safe."

Emma raised her eyebrows. "So they're okay?"

"Yes."

Cole watched the tension immediately drop from Emma's shoulders.

"But they aren't answering when I call," she said after a moment.

"Why don't we sit down and talk?"

Cole and Volker stepped aside to let Newman farther into the room. He walked over and stood in front of a club chair. After a moment's hesitation, Emma dropped down on the nearby sofa and then the sergeant also took a seat. Cole positioned himself on the sofa so that he was between Emma and Newman. Volker remained standing where he could keep watch out the front window. Even if they got some answers right now, that still didn't guarantee that Emma was safe.

"First of all, I heard about the kidnapping attempt. Are you all right?"

Emma shook off the question as if it were irrelevant. "Why did witness security come for my parents? Why *now*?" She took a breath and when she spoke again she sounded slightly calmer. "What happened?"

"Royce Walker was finally tracked down in northern California and he's under arrest. So of course that means the trial will be resumed."

Cole watched Emma's face blanch and her jaw went slack. "Who is Royce Walker?" Cole asked.

"He's a high-powered criminal gang leader in Los Angeles," Newman said when Emma seemed unable to speak for a moment. "Some of his gang members helped him escape custody just before his murder trial was slated to begin a year after his arrest. He's been on the run ever since. Well, until roughly twenty-four hours ago when he finally got caught."

"My dad saw the murder happen," Emma said as she turned to Cole. "He wanted to testify because he thought it was the right thing to do. I was fifteen at the time, and I remember the cops watching our house round-the-clock. We figured once Dad testified, any threat to him would be over. Then Walker escaped and the authorities reasoned my dad was even more vulnerable as a potential witness. They said there was an even greater chance that Walker's gang would come after him. Or that Walker himself might try to kill my dad to prevent his testimony. That's when we went into witness protection."

Cole was stunned. All this time he'd known Emma and he had no idea about any of this. He turned to Newman. "So why are you here?"

"I'm on the local task force that works with federal witness security when they're in this region. I got the call to watch this house until the team could get here, though I didn't have any specifics on what was happening at the time." He turned his attention to Emma. "Martel asked me to follow up on Emma and her brother once their parents were safely out of the area. Now that the children are no longer minors, security is focused mainly on the government witness and his spouse."

"So Austin isn't with my parents?"

Newman shook his head. "He is not. Do you know where he might be?"

"I don't." A note of panic crept into her voice. "I guess he officially lives here, but he's got a couple of friends from high school who moved into their own place shortly after they all graduated last June and he stays with them a lot."

"Let these friends know that if they're protecting him, they need to step up and contact me," Newman said firmly. He pulled out a business card and extended it toward Emma.

Emma ignored the contact card Newman was trying to offer her. "What are you talking about?" she demanded, crossing her arms. "Given what's happening Austin *needs* someone to protect him."

Newman blew out a breath and set the card on the arm

of his chair. "It looks as if your brother is the person who gave away your parents' location to Walker's gang. Sold them the information, possibly. He's the reason they knew your dad was here in Cedar Lodge."

Cole watched Emma's body tense. Her jawline firmed and anger seemed to come off her in waves. "That is absolutely ridiculous."

"According to Martel, Austin very much resented the move up here from Los Angeles and he held on to that resentment for a long time."

"He was *ten years old* when we moved. He had to give up his friends and his school and everything he knew. Of course he was angry."

For a moment no one spoke.

Emma checked her phone again, as if someone might have called or texted and she hadn't noticed. "I don't believe this," she muttered.

"It's not like I'm looking to arrest your brother," Newman said. "He isn't officially a criminal suspect, and I haven't been tasked to bring him back to the station. But I would like him to confirm that he's responsible for the security breach. It helps with integrity of the whole witness protection system if we can understand how security failures happen. I'd appreciate your help."

"And I *want* to help you." Emma lifted her chin. "I want you to know that Austin isn't responsible."

"Okay." Newman nodded. "In the meantime, I can take you to a safe house out of town where you won't be vulnerable to another attack like the one today."

She shook her head. "No, thank you. I'm going to stay in Cedar Lodge and I'm going to find my brother and then we can get everything cleared up. I need to make sure

Austin is safe and I need to talk to my parents and make sure they're okay, too."

"What about your own safety?" Cole turned to her. "Maybe you should take him up on his offer. It looks to me like the criminals came to get your dad so he couldn't testify and when they couldn't get to him they went after you instead. Sadly, criminals the world over control their target victims by grabbing family members and threatening to harm them. The plan is likely to grab you or Austin and threaten to hurt you if your dad goes through with his plan to give his witness testimony. The kidnappers have a job to do and they're going to come after you again."

"They might already have Austin," Emma said softly. She sighed and the starch appeared to go out of her backbone. "If my parents are in protective custody and I'm hiding in some other town, who's going to help my brother?"

"How are you going to help him if you're in danger?" Cole asked. Even with her grit and determination to fight against her attackers, Emma likely wouldn't have escaped abduction on her own.

"What kind of life would I have if I walked away from my family and only worried about myself?" she responded. "Would you ever do that?"

Cole didn't have any siblings, but he did have family members and friends he cared about. And no, he would not abandon them if they were in danger. Not even if that meant putting himself at risk.

He understood how Emma felt. Fear for her safety tied a knot in Cole's stomach. Emma was going to stay in Cedar Lodge until she found her brother, and she was going to be in danger the whole time.

Cole would not let her go through this alone.

* * *

"You didn't have to stay," Emma said to Cole in the waiting area of the urgent care clinic after she'd seen a doctor.

Not that she was surprised he had waited. She'd worked with Cole enough to know that he had a strong sense of ethics and responsibility. Even if he wasn't always personable.

Okay, maybe that was unfair. He was friendly to a point but then also politely aloof. That was why, three years after meeting him, Cole was still somewhat of a mystery. But she was nevertheless grateful for the concern he was showing her now.

Shortly after Sergeant Newman had confirmed Emma's parents were safe and then turned around and accused her younger brother of selling information about their family's location to the bad guys, the conversation at her parents' house had died down. Newman left and Volker had reminded Emma and Cole that he needed them down at the police station for official statements. After he gave them a ride back to Cole's truck at the crime scene, Cole had insisted on driving Emma to the clinic to get her collarbone x-rayed before they reported to the station.

In the waiting area Cole got to his feet. Behind him, rain splattered against the window. When storms rolled into the narrow river valley where Cedar Lodge was located, they typically rolled in *fast*. It was one of the many things that was substantially different from the desert-like Southern California town where Emma had come from.

"What did the doctor say?" Cole asked.

"No fracture, just a moderate bone bruise. Over-the-counter pain meds and try to take it easy." Her collarbone was really starting to ache, too. The adrenaline rush after the kidnapping had bottomed out and now Emma felt shaky and tired. She looked at Cole, recalling that he'd worked an overnight shift before arriving at the crash scene and then searching for her. "How long have you been awake?" she asked.

He offered her a half shrug and declined to answer.

"Why don't you go home and get some rest?" she added. "I can get a rideshare back to my car."

"I'll make sure your car gets back to your apartment," he said, deflecting her question. "Right now let me drive you to the police station. I've already gotten a text from Volker asking for an estimate of when we'll get there. I told him to calm down."

Emma knew that Cole, Kris Volker and sheriff's deputy Dylan Ruiz had been friends for a long enough time that the interaction between them tended to be more informal. The three of them were absolute professionals, but there were moments when they weren't above teasing or mildly harassing one another.

"I got a text from a coworker at the library asking what happened to me." Emma shook her head. "I can't believe I completely forgot about work. I didn't give a lot of detail in my reply. Just told her something very serious had come up and I would be in touch later."

"Good. Until things get figured out, it's probably best to give out as little information as possible."

"That's what I thought." She glanced out at the rain. "Ready to make a run for it?"

Cole pulled off his fire department jacket and offered it to her.

"That's okay. I won't melt in the rain."

"Take it. Please."

Rather than make an issue of it, she nodded. "Okay. Thanks."

He stepped around to put it on her shoulders. "Probably best if you don't move your arms around too much right now."

"No argument there." Moving her arms triggered the ache in her collarbone.

Rather than heading out the door, he hesitated for a moment, looking into her eyes.

"What?" she asked.

"I thought of something while I was sitting here. You didn't tell Sergeant Newman about the man you saw behind your parents' house."

"Oh." No, she hadn't. "With my thoughts going off in so many different directions, I didn't think of it. But I'll let him know." Newman's card was still on the arm of the chair back at the house. She'd call or text him after they were finished at the police station.

"Do you think the person you saw could have been your brother?" Cole asked.

Emma shook her head. "No. I'd know Austin if I saw him. And if he saw me, he'd come talk to me. He wouldn't run away." She started for the exit and then stopped, struggling to contain a flare of anger. "Wait, are you asking me that because you think I saw Austin and I was trying to hide that fact?"

"I had to ask," Cole said mildly.

"Well, now you have." She clamped her mouth shut and exhaled audibly through her nose.

It couldn't have been Austin, could it?

She resumed walking toward the exit, tired and annoyed and angry and sore.

And *scared*. For her parents, especially her dad, who was going to have to testify in open court against a stone-cold killer. And for her brother, who might have already been taken captive by the bad guys. If the thugs had watched and planned how to best get at Emma, why wouldn't they have done the same with Austin, too?

It was just past one o'clock in the afternoon, but the heavy clouds and rain made their surroundings appear dusky and filled with shadows. The clinic and its adjoining parking lot were near the edge of Bear Lake, and right now Emma could barely even see the surface of the water. Chilled, she flicked up the collar on Cole's jacket as she stepped in unavoidable puddles on the way to his truck.

Bang!

They were almost to the pickup when a gunshot cracked across the parking lot, immediately followed by two more shots.

Cole hollered, "Gun! Get down!"

Emma dropped to the pavement near the truck's passenger door, wincing at the pain in her collarbone caused by the sudden movement.

Cole had taken cover near the tailgate, using the SUV parked beside them as a shield. In a squatting position, while staying low and taking a look around, he grabbed his radio from his belt and keyed the mic. "Shots fired at the urgent care center on Glacier Street!"

Emma didn't hear the response. One moment she was staring down at asphalt that was covered with rainwater, and the next moment someone came up from behind and threw a blanket over her head. The assailant yanked her to her feet and started dragging her backward, and she dropped her bag with her phone in it.

Shock and panic disoriented her so that she was unable scream. She could barely even breathe. When she finally took in a breath to yell for Cole, the damp fabric covering her face was drawn into her mouth and she could only make a muffled sound.

Bang! Bang!

Gunfire started up again as Emma felt her feet scrape the asphalt and she got dragged through the mud and grass and pine needles along a downward slope toward the lake.

What was the assailant planning to do? *Drown her?*

Was Cole okay or had he been shot?

She lifted her feet, hoping that carrying her full weight would slow the attacker down. But she was a small woman and the assailant was obviously strong because the move made no difference.

As they moved closer to the water she heard an outboard motor. Was a boater passing nearby? Maybe whoever was piloting the watercraft would help her. Having learned her lesson moments ago, this time she turned her head aside before drawing in a deep breath and screaming, followed by repeated cries of "Help!"

She dropped her feet back down and kicked at her assailant's legs and tried to stomp his instep and trip up his footing. He stumbled slightly but kept dragging her along.

The sound of the outboard motor grew louder and then she suddenly found herself ankle-deep in cold lake water.

Two more gunshots fired, followed by the sound of someone running.

Emma was dragged farther out into the water, shoved against the side of a boat, and then lifted and pushed the rest of the way in.

She flailed her arms and immediately felt a blow to the side of her head, stunning her. The attacker who'd grabbed her climbed into the boat with her. It sounded like the person she'd heard running jumped in with them, too.

Cold terror shot through her. Bear Lake was a sprawling body of water lined with numerous coves and inlets where the criminals could easily hide until they could make a clean getaway.

If the thugs escaped with Emma now, Cole and the cops would never find them.

Most likely, nobody would ever find *her*.

FOUR

Cole desperately tried to focus in several directions at once. Emma's scream had yanked his attention toward the lake, but he still needed to know where the shooter was and he also had to listen for sounds of anyone approaching that he was not yet aware of.

The rain was falling harder, making it more difficult for him to see and hear. He didn't have a weapon and he would be going up against at least one gunman. The shooter hadn't fired off any rounds in the last couple of minutes, and it seemed a reasonable assumption the attacker had moved through the strip of trees and down to the lake where Emma's scream had originated.

Cole grabbed his phone and punched in the numbers. "9-1-1, what is your emergency?"

He recognized the dispatcher's voice. "Lana, it's Cole. I'm under fire at the urgent care clinic parking lot on Glacier Street. I came here with Emma Hayes and now someone's grabbed her." He'd been crouched on the other side of the truck and hadn't seen it happen, but it was obvious she'd been abducted. Looking around now he could see tracks in the mud that disappeared into the band of trees between the pavement and Bear Lake. "They're headed toward the lake. I'm going after them."

Lana began to ask a follow-up question in her calm, professional way but Cole disconnected. He understood that she'd want him to stay on the line and continue with updates, but there were only so many things he could do at one time. Right now he was determined to press through the pine trees and down to the lake's edge without being spotted so he could get to Emma.

Having a gun would have made things easier.

The first couple of years after he'd returned home from his final deployment, he'd kept a pistol either on him or in his vehicle. He'd been used to carrying a sidearm, and it made him feel prepared to take whatever action was needed. But as time went by, *not* carrying a gun whenever he left home felt like he was releasing an old burden and embracing freedom.

At the moment that all seemed foolish.

He reached the last of the trees at the edge of the shoreline and saw two thugs and Emma in a boat with an outboard motor. For the sake of convenience, plenty of people left the key in the ignition of small inexpensive boats like this one, especially when they were moored to private docks.

The two kidnappers wore jackets with the hoods pulled over their heads, mostly covering their faces. Their physical builds and clothes looked similar to the attackers who had grabbed Emma earlier.

These people were relentless. Could be their own lives were in danger if they didn't complete the job their criminal boss had assigned them.

One of the attackers, apparently the shooter since he held a gun in one hand, settled at the stern by the motor ready to pilot the boat. The other kidnapper was near the bow, struggling to contain Emma as she fought with him and clawed aside a ratty-looking blanket that had covered her head.

Cole assumed the thug manhandling Emma had a gun tucked away somewhere, too.

Now that he knew her story and that her father's trial testimony would put a powerful criminal in prison for life, he was fairly certain they wouldn't immediately kill Emma but rather kidnap her and use her as a bargaining chip.

Nevertheless, he couldn't let them take her away.

He took a quick glance behind him, up the hill toward the parking lot. Even with the strip of pine trees in the way, he should still see at least flickers of red and blue emergency lights if help had arrived. He would have expected to hear sirens, even if it was just a sound blip in the distance before the cops decided to opt for a stealth approach. He didn't see or hear anything.

Cole was on his own.

Surprise was the only advantage and potential weapon Cole had to draw on. He would do what he could to make the best of it.

He untied his heavy work boots and set them aside, tossing his phone into one of them. Then he broke from the cover of the trees and ran for the water, yelling *"Stop!"* He waved his arms and did his best to look panicked and witless while hoping and praying he didn't get shot. He figured he had a fairly decent chance. Hitting a moving target, in shadowy conditions and when you were taken by surprise, wasn't easy. Not even if you spent time in target practice every day. He knew that from experience.

Both assailants looked in his direction. The jerk holding Emma, Bald Guy from the car crash attack, quickly turned his attention back to her as she struggled to break free. The kidnapper at the outboard motor pointed his gun at Cole and fired just before Cole reached the waterline. The navy veteran changed his trajectory so he was still headed into the lake but at an angle away from the boat. He wanted it to look like he was in a blind panic to get away from the bullets and danger.

Apparently, his ruse worked. The criminal didn't bother to fire any more rounds in his direction and turned his attention back to the boat motor, leaning toward it as if he needed to adjust something.

Cole quickly reached deeper water, filled his lungs with air, and then dove down. He immediately changed direction and swam back toward the stern of the boat. As soon as he reached the motor he looked up through the water at the assailant above him and then shot up out of the water and grabbed the criminal's lower arm.

The criminal, Ponytail Guy from the earlier kidnapping attempt, faltered in shocked surprise. Cole quickly took a breath of air while also pressing his foot against the side of the boat for added leverage. With his free hand he reached up and grabbed the thug's other arm, completely throwing the man off-balance, and now Cole was finally able to yank him overboard.

Ignoring the creep flailing in the water behind him, Cole dived back underwater and swam toward the bow of the boat. Looking up through the clear lake water he could see that Emma and the attacker were still struggling. Cole began to surface for a breath of air when the assailant spotted him and fired into the lake.

Cole dove back down and away, waiting for as long as he could before surfacing for another breath. When he lifted his head out of the water, he spotted the kidnapper he'd already tossed into the lake awkwardly trying to swim back to the boat. He reached the side but was unable to pull himself up and into it.

Turning his attention back to Emma, Cole was gratified to see that she was still fighting her kidnapper. Meanwhile, the assailant in the water had started yelling to his partner for help.

Emma was a small woman, and the jerk holding her was able to drag her wherever he wanted to, even though she was kicking and twisting and biting. He dragged her toward the side of the boat closest to his criminal companion.

Emma's efforts weren't having much impact in terms of physically harming the thug, but she was a huge distraction as Bald Guy tried to fish his fellow kidnapper out of the water.

Distraction was exactly what Cole needed. He pulled himself up into the boat behind Emma and her attacker, unseen as well as unheard over the shouts of Ponytail Guy still slapping at the water along with the loud growl of the diesel outboard motor.

Cole rushed forward and reached for the gun in Bald Guy's hand, but the thug somehow sensed Cole was there and jerked his hand away just as Cole reached for the weapon. Cole's hand knocked against the gun and the pistol tumbled out of the criminal's hand, ending up on the deck several feet away.

Bald Guy tried to turn toward Cole, but Emma fought against the assailant, twisting and stomping on his feet. Her flailing efforts gave Cole the opportunity he needed to throw a powerful punch directly into the center of Bald Guy's face. Cole followed it up with a left hook that sent the criminal spinning and gave Emma a chance to finally break free of the kidnapper's grasp.

Cole made a move for the gun still lying on the deck, but Bald Guy was closer and he lurched toward the weapon to grab it.

At the stern of the boat, Ponytail Guy had finally pulled himself back onto the deck.

Stand and fight was generally Cole's first instinct, but he was aware that it wasn't always the smartest option. It didn't look like the best choice right now.

Beside him, Emma breathed heavily and looked around frantically, her eyes widened with fear and what looked like the leading edge of panic.

"You know how to swim, right?" Cole asked.

She nodded.

"We need to get in the water. *Now.*"

"Okay."

They rushed to the side of the boat facing the shore and jumped off.

Cole hit the water and opened his eyes before he surfaced to check on Emma. She was already swimming fast toward the shoreline. It looked like she was used to being in the water. When he lifted his head above the surface for a breath of air, he heard sirens.

Bang! Bang!

Gunshots from the boat behind them hit the water between him and Emma. Had the thugs decided they'd rather have Emma dead or was this just frustration and rage? He had no way of knowing, so he just swam closer to her, staying behind to provide the best shield he could between Emma and the shooters.

He risked a quick glance back as the boat roared away.

Back toward shore, blue lights were visible through the clusters of trees at the edge of the lake. Cops had made it to the parking lot where Cole's truck was parked. He and

Emma were walking up out of the water when he spotted two officers racing toward them.

Emma was moving unsteadily and she dropped down into a sitting position on the mixture of sand and wild grass. Cole sat beside her. She leaned into him and he wrapped an arm around her shoulders while they waited for the cops to approach and question them. Cole kept his gaze focused on the lake. The kidnappers had already disappeared around a bend in the shoreline, but that didn't mean that Emma was safe. The criminals coming after her were shockingly determined, but Cole was equally determined that he would keep Emma from being their victim.

Emma sat on a wooden bench in the women's locker room at the fire station and took a moment to collect her thoughts. The police who'd arrived at the lake had peppered her and Cole with questions before radioing for a police patrol boat and setting out to search for the attackers. After that, Cole had repeatedly asked her how she was and how her collarbone felt as they made the drive to the fire station. The answer was that she was fine but her collarbone ached.

Both she and Cole kept an extra set of clothes and pair of shoes in their lockers, which was standard practice for all the emergency responders since you never knew what might happen in the course of working a shift. She'd just now finished changing into dry clothes.

The firehouse was next to the police station, and Cole's cop friend Kris was waiting to walk the two of them over there so he could finish taking their statements.

She'd recovered her dropped phone from the parking lot and was holding it now. She looked down at the unbroken screen, grateful that her EMT job had prompted her to keep the device in a sturdy case.

She had a voicemail from her mother asking her to call back as soon as possible. It was such a relief to hear her mom's voice that Emma almost burst into tears. She also had a missed call from her brother, but he hadn't left a message. She sent him a text again asking him to call her. She was the big sister. Austin, despite the tough-guy attitude he sometimes displayed, was just an eighteen-year-old kid. At least in her mind he was a kid. She didn't know what kind of situation he was in, and she hoped her own edgy emotional state after the attacks didn't make him feel even more fearful or panicked when they finally spoke.

After a prayer for help with organizing her thoughts, Emma called her mom. She'd already decided not to tell her about the attacks. She would eventually, but right now her parents had enough on their plates.

Gina Hayes picked up after the first ring. "Honey!"

"Mom." Despite her best efforts, Emma started to cry.

"Are you all right?" Her mother sounded panicked. "Your dad is right here, let me put this on Speaker."

"Hi, sweetie." Neil Hayes's voice coming through the phone felt like a warming sip of tea. The man's ability to stay calm under the most trying of situations was amazing.

Emma cleared her throat and tried to sound happier. "I'm so glad to finally hear from you guys. I was so worried."

"Yeah, well, they hustled us out to the county airport and onto one flight and then another, and we didn't get an opportunity to call until a short while ago. I couldn't believe they wouldn't wait for us to call you and your brother so we could all leave together, but according to the witness protection people you and Austin have aged out of the program and you're on your own." Mom didn't sound happy about that.

"You're all right?" Emma asked.

"We're okay," Dad said. "Your mother and I are more worried about you and your brother. We think you two should leave town."

"You've talked to Austin?" Emma asked cautiously.

"We have," Mom said. "And your brother's got it in his head that he's responsible for our location being discovered. You need to talk him out of thinking that."

"We know he got in touch online with some friends shortly after we moved to Cedar Lodge," Dad said. "We learned about it years ago. He told us he never gave away the name of the town and we believe him."

"It's just as likely our fault as his," Mom interjected. "The truth is your dad and I stayed in touch with your grandparents and aunts and uncles even though we weren't supposed to. And Dad and I just agreed that we need to let your brother know about that."

Emma felt her eyes go wide. As kids, their parents' rule had been for no one in the family to connect with anybody from their old life. Not even relatives.

"It just felt like we were being punished for your dad doing the right thing and agreeing to testify," Mom continued. "When this first started we thought we'd only be cut off from everybody for a year or two at most. After four years we decided that was enough and we got in touch with everybody. Maybe your dad or I accidently let slip information that we shouldn't have. Maybe a relative told somebody something and somehow the information got back to the Walker criminal gang." She sighed heavily.

"I don't know. But I do know we can't let your brother take on the responsibility for our cover getting blown."

Emma rubbed her eyes. "I just messaged Austin to call me. Maybe you could encourage him to hurry up and do that. When we get together we'll call you and see what we want to do next. If we want to go down to California with you two or go somewhere else."

Emma heard a voice in the background on the other end of the call.

"We've got to go for now," Mom said. "Love you."

"Love you, too," Dad added.

"I'll find Austin," Emma promised, just before the call ended.

After taking a few moments to collect her thoughts, Emma walked out of the locker room to the adjoining crew room where she smelled a fresh pot of coffee brewing. Cole stood waiting. When he looked at Emma, she felt her stomach give a nervous twist. As if she were attracted to him.

This is Cole, she told herself. *The guy you've worked with for two years. Come on.* He was just Cole. Not some man she had a romantic interest in.

Yes, he'd been courageous and amazing, not only most recently at the lake but actually starting with him saving her from the kidnappers earlier this morning.

People have tried to kidnap me twice today. For a moment the sheer bizarreness of that reality slowed down her thoughts. Her gaze had shifted away from her part-time work partner, but now she looked at him again. That feeling of nervous, fluttery attraction was still there. It even ratcheted up a notch when his initial expression of hardened determination softened into concern as he looked at her. Then he turned and reached into a nearby cabinet to grab a mug. "I know you're not yourself without *plenty* of coffee and I need you to stay on your toes." He filled the mug. "You want your usual ridiculous amount of cream and sugar?"

It was no different from their regular banter. Just a co-worker offering to get her coffee. So why did his offer to get her coffee now elicit a warm feeling that felt very *personal*?

This had to be some weird emotional aftereffect, like shock. It was a chemical response to extreme stress added to emotions that had already been pushed to their limit. That was all it was.

"Most people like their coffee to taste good," she said, continuing their usual banter, understanding that he was trying to create a moment of normalcy for the both of them and appreciating the effort. "You take your coffee so bitter I don't know why you don't just chew the grounds."

Cole laughed while adding cream and sugar to her coffee and then handed it to her.

After a couple of sips, Emma told him she'd spoken to her parents and that they were okay. "I still need to find my brother, though," she said. "When I do, we'll probably leave town."

Cole leaned his back against the counter. "Sounds like a good idea."

Kris Volker walked into the crew room from the firehouse bay where the fire trucks and ambulances were parked. "You two are certainly magnets for trouble today."

"I'd rather not be," Emma said before taking a sip of coffee.

Volker gave her a sympathetic look. "Unfortunately, we don't have either of the attackers in custody. We found the boat, but they weren't in it. The search for the criminals is our top priority right now. Let's get your official statements taken care of, do an extended interview, see if there's some detail you can recall that will give us a new lead."

Emma looked down at the last of her coffee. The surface was rippling as a result of her shaking hands. Adrenaline, fear, or maybe both. The violent criminals were still at large hunting for her and probably for her brother, too. Was Austin someplace safe? She didn't know.

Emma rinsed her mug and put it in the dishwasher. Cole did the same thing.

"Let's go," Emma said. The truth was she was terrified to step out of the safety of the fire station. But as she'd very recently learned, you couldn't hide forever. She would take whatever risks were necessary to help the cops capture the kidnappers and find her brother before it was too late.

FIVE

"I'm sorry all of this is happening to you," Police Chief Gerald Ellis said to Emma as she took a seat in a small conference room at the police station.

"Thank you."

Cole was there, along with Kris Volker and Detective Sam Campbell, who had been introduced to Emma in the squad room a few moments ago.

"First off, Sergeant Newman from the sheriff's department contacted me and said that he thinks your brother might somehow be involved with the criminal gang that's come after you. He believes Austin might have sold them information on your family's location here in Cedar Lodge. It's something to consider as we work to solve these crimes against you. Do you have any thoughts on that?"

"Yeah, I think it's ridiculous. If information about our location got out through any member of my family, it was by accident. I'm sure of that."

"Well, I am concerned about his safety. These thugs might try to kidnap him, too. Do you know where we could find him?"

She shook her head. "I'm trying to get in touch with him because *I'm* worried about him."

She'd moved out of her parents' house and begun supporting herself three years ago. Her relationship with Austin hadn't been especially close lately. They were five years apart and that felt like a big gap when one of you was a teenager still living at home and the other was out living an independent life. Emma looked down at her nails for a moment to collect herself before she burst into tears.

She *should* have kept an eye on her brother. Over the last few months, after he'd graduated high school and turned eighteen, she should have made more of an effort to find something in common with him. An arrow of guilt speared her heart when she remembered the few times he'd reached out to her to meet for lunch or go to a movie or something and she'd told him she didn't have time.

"He has a couple of friends he sometimes stays with for a few days at a time. I'm going to talk to them. And I think he still has a job at Burger Bonanza. I'm going to look for him there, too."

"I want to emphasize that he's not wanted by police at this time, but there may come a point when it's important for us to talk with him. And I would like to know that he's okay."

Emma nodded. "I'll let you know when I finally talk to him."

"Thank you. Meanwhile, let's talk about our investigation into the attacks on you. River Patrol just found what we believe is the boat used by the attackers." Ellis glanced at Campbell. The detective tapped the screen of the tablet in front of him and then slid it across the table toward Emma and Cole.

"That's it, that's the boat." It appeared abandoned, untethered, and drifting near the lakeshore.

Cole nodded in agreement.

Campbell pulled the tablet back toward himself. "Stolen and later ditched not far from the location of your attack."

Which indicated to Emma that the assailants were likely somewhere in town since the attack had been near Glacier Street and the downtown area.

"This would be a good time for Officer Volker to complete his reports." Chief Ellis looked at Volker and the patrol officer opened a document on his laptop.

"I've already got a lot of the basic information I need," Volker said. "What I'm looking for now is a narrative of what happened."

He started with Emma, and then it was Cole's turn. The chief and detective both listened closely to the descriptions of what exactly had happened.

"Did either of the kidnappers look familiar to you?" the detective asked after they were finished, his glance taking in both Emma and Cole.

"No," Emma said.

"Never seen them before," Cole added.

Campbell settled his focus on Emma. "In the last week or so, have you noticed anyone unusual hanging around your home? Have you felt like you were being watched? Did either of your parents mention anything odd happening to them? If so, perhaps we could track down video footage from near the location where it happened."

"I haven't had any experience like that and my parents didn't mention anything." Emma rubbed her hands over her arms. It was a chilling thought that someone might have been stalking her or her family for days and they'd had no idea.

"All right," Campbell said, tapping the screen on his notebook again. "I have one more thing to ask of you. Take a look at these mug shots and see if you recognize any of them. Most are locals who have either a history of violence or criminal connections that make us think they could be the attackers. There are some mixed in that were sent to us from detectives down in Los Angeles. These would be known associates of the criminal your dad will be testifying against in California."

Emma began swiping the photos with Cole also looking at the screen. No one looked familiar. Cole agreed.

"Now what?" Emma asked. "Do I just wait and hope they don't attack me again before you can find them?"

"We've got other avenues of investigation," Chief Ellis said. "Detective Campbell and his team will be talking to confidential informants. They'll also try to track down security video from locations near where the boat was stolen, as well as where the kidnappers stole the car they had earlier this morning and see what they can learn from that. We'll be checking local hotels and campgrounds, too, since the thugs have to stay somewhere." He glanced at Kris Volker. "Until we have identifying photos of the attackers it'll be hard to have patrol officers on the lookout for the criminals, but we can beef up patrols around your home."

Ellis tapped the keyboard of his laptop. "Looks like you live at Lakeside Terrace."

"It's a pretty secure building," Emma said. At least she'd always felt that way about the four-floor craftsman-style structure. But then she'd never had anyone trying to kidnap her before. "Keycard locks at the two main entrances and for the elevators and video cameras in the hallways."

"None of that would keep out a professional who's determined to get to you," the chief said grimly. "But that could be true of virtually any place you would stay in town. I encourage you to remain vigilant. Make sure your doors and windows are locked. Don't open the door for anyone you don't know."

"And maybe sleep in the living room so if someone does get in through the front door you'll hear them," Volker added.

Emma was scared all over again. Part of her wanted to flee to safety, to take off and hide someplace hundreds or thousands of miles away. But a stronger part of her absolutely would not abandon her brother. And she stubbornly didn't want to be forced to start a new life in a new place all over again.

Maybe the friendships she'd developed in Cedar Lodge weren't based on her telling people the *entire* truth about her past. But the relationships and emotional connections were real. And in the end, didn't everybody hold back a little bit of something of themselves from other people? Not to be deceitful but simply because they felt more comfortable that way?

"I don't know what else to advise you," Ellis added. "Going into hiding on your own would not be easy. And it would be expensive. I wish I could offer you a personal round-the-clock bodyguard but right now I just don't have the staffing or budget to do that."

"I intend to spend as much time with her as possible," Cole interjected. "If you're all right with that," he added as Emma turned to him.

She was more than all right with it. But she simply said, "Thank you." Hopefully the whole situation would be resolved quickly. For everyone's physical safety and so she and Cole could get back to their normal working relationship. Because with her life in danger, and her brother at risk, too, the last thing she needed was to be distracted by this unsettling new attraction to Cole.

Ellis got to his feet and everyone else followed suit. "We're going to get back to work," he said to Emma and Cole. "Call 9-1-1 immediately if you have any concerns. Beyond that, I suggest you both get some rest."

They filed out of the conference room, Emma walking alongside Cole. "I'm tired, but I'm also too amped to go home and sit around just yet," she said. "How about you take me to get my SUV from my parents' house? After that I can stop to get something to eat on my way home." She would have anticipated a loss of appetite after all that had happened today, but that wasn't the case.

"I'll follow you two just to make sure no one's waiting to ambush Emma," Volker said, having overheard while walking behind them.

"Good idea," Cole commented.

They stepped outside and Emma glanced at the nearby street as they walked the short distance back to the fire station where Cole's truck was parked. She needed to grab her duffel bag with her wet clothes, too, so she could take them home. Maybe something mundane like doing laundry would help settle her nerves.

In the early days after her dad had witnessed Royce Walker committing murder in a Los Angeles alleyway, Emma had been vigilant in taking note of her surroundings. Over time that compulsion had faded, but now here it was again. She wondered if her family would ever be safe. Maybe the attacks weren't ever going to stop. At least not until the criminals got what they wanted and silenced her dad by harming him or kidnapping a member of his family.

I have to start carrying a gun.

Cole glanced into his rearview mirror at Kris in his

patrol car on their way to retrieve Emma's SUV. The cop wouldn't be able to keep an eye on Emma all the time, and Cole was committed now to stepping up and protecting Emma as best he could.

Cole didn't have a problem with guns, it was just that he hadn't ever imagined needing to carry one around town for the sake of keeping a companion and himself alive. When he left the military, he'd wanted to continue to use his skills as a medic. When his mother became terminally ill while he was in high school, they'd moved to his grandfather's ranch and Cole had helped take care of his mom. Hearing about some of the activities of his criminal father, there'd been times when Cole wanted to become a cop and hunt down thieving, violent, drug-dealing thugs like his old man and lock them up. Make the world a better place. But in the end, going out to rescue people who were injured or seriously ill and helping them felt more like his true calling.

At the moment, it looked as if his life needed to contain a mixture of both those types of action. Keep his job as a paramedic and be an armed bodyguard for Emma.

He glanced over at her seated beside him, taken aback at the drive he felt to care for her and protect her. Earlier in the day, he'd told himself that he was motivated to help out a coworker and fellow member of his community. But in truth, this was something more and it had come at him unexpectedly.

Cole had been engaged once. A long-distance relationship that was probably a bad idea from the start. Both of them had been serving in the military, and they didn't have much actual time together in person until they both returned to civilian life and each got an apartment in San Diego where they could spend some quality time together while getting ready for their wedding, which would be a year away.

The relationship fizzled. It just did. There wasn't a big blow out over a specific problem, there was just the simple fact that they each had expectations about the other that didn't match reality. After it ended, Cole moved back to Cedar Lodge. It was something he'd wanted to do, anyway. He'd dated some very nice women, but nothing had *clicked*. He hadn't been able to imagine a future with any of those women.

Now, with Emma, maybe he could imagine that.

Whoa, wait. Where had *that* come from? Cole couldn't let himself think like that because Emma was eight years younger than him and they worked together and, well, it just didn't make any sense.

"I'm going to call Shari at the main city library and see if she'll come by my apartment to pick up the books I was supposed to deliver and get them out to the Meadowlark branch library," Emma said.

Cole turned to her and laughed, grateful to have his thoughts redirected.

"What?" Emma demanded.

"After everything you've been through today, you're still worried about those books?"

"People want to read them," she said emphatically. "They cared enough to *request* them. It's my job to get books into people's hands, especially people who can't get to the main library and who might not have the ability or desire to read books in a digital format."

He couldn't keep the smile from his face. "I admire your commitment." He meant it.

They reached her parents' house, and Cole pulled up into the driveway behind Emma's SUV.

The moment for humor was gone, and Cole became especially alert to their surroundings.

Emma started to open her door.

"Let's wait for Kris to have a look around first," Cole said, watching his friend pull up behind them. "He'll want to make sure the kidnappers aren't nearby."

"Doesn't seem likely they are."

"Better to check and know for certain."

Emma gave him a thoughtful look before digging into her bag for her keys and car fob and then holding them toward him. "The silver-colored key unlocks the front door."

Cole opened his door, got out and handed the keys to Kris. "Silver key for the front door. I'd go with you to search the house but I don't want to leave Emma alone."

"I can see that," Kris said in a teasing tone.

Cole glared at him. "Somebody's got to stay with her and make sure she's safe."

Kris held his hands up. "I'm not criticizing." He flashed a grin that only lasted a few seconds before his features became more serious. He drew his service weapon and went to check around Emma's SUV and then inside the house.

Cole kept his attention focused on the house while Kris was inside, listening for any sounds of trouble. Emma appeared to do the same thing, as they sat together in tense silence.

Kris finally exited the house and slid his gun back into the holster. "Doesn't look like anybody's been in there since we left," he said as he walked up to Cole's window. "I'm going to get back on patrol."

"Thank you," Emma said, finally getting out of the truck as Kris drove away.

"Do you want to go straight home while I go get you

something to eat?" Cole called out to Emma through his rolled-down window.

"I'd rather just pick something up now and go home. As soon as I eat I want to climb into bed and hide there for a while. I'm hoping Austin will call soon and I can get him to come to my apartment."

"Fair enough. What do you want to eat?"

"A sandwich and some German potato salad from Dill Pickle Deli sounds good. That okay with you?"

"Sure, whatever you want."

Emma got into her SUV. Cole backed out and then had her get in front of him so he could watch her and make sure she was okay while they started toward the center of town. As he drove, he hoped and prayed they wouldn't come under attack again before he could see her safely home.

SIX

"I got the chocolate coffee sugar bomb you asked for." Cole stepped into Emma's apartment the next morning carrying her double-shot mocha, his own brewed coffee with a splash of cream, and a bag with fresh bagels and small containers of whipped cream cheese.

"Thanks." The word came out scratchy, matching Emma's rough appearance.

"Looks like you didn't get much rest last night." They'd exchanged texts before Cole left the ranch this morning and he already knew that Emma hadn't yet heard from Austin.

Emma closed the door behind him and bolted it. She pulled her drink from the cardboard carrier and offered him a mocking glare. "I suppose you think *you* look fresh as a daisy."

The banter was a good sign. She was acting like her normal self, which was significant given all she'd been through in the last twenty-four hours.

"I feel rested," Cole said. "Fell into bed as soon as I got back to the ranch and was instantly asleep." He'd been awake for well over twenty-four hours at that point. The adrenaline spikes and anxiety as a result of the attacks hadn't been enough to overcome his need for solid rest.

"Yeah, well, I pictured my brother in some kind of horrible, dangerous situation every time I closed my eyes. Wasn't doing it intentionally, it just happened. When I did fall asleep, I had nightmares about him that woke me up." She took a sip of her coffee, quickly followed by two more. "Thank you. This is perfect."

"I told them to put in double the normal amount of chocolate syrup."

A slight smile broke through her scowl. "Good call." She looked inside the white bag he'd brought, then picked it up and headed toward a toaster oven on her kitchen counter.

Cole glanced around. Her apartment was on the third of four floors. Beside the dining area, a glass door opened onto a balcony and beyond that he could see sunlight sparkling on the surface of Bear Lake. "You really have a nice view." He'd been here yesterday, after seeing her home, but the curtains had been closed.

"I've been happy here," Emma said over her shoulder as she split the bagels and started them toasting.

Cole walked toward her, noticing that the place looked immaculate and smelled faintly of lemon. When he reached the kitchen, he spotted several household cleaners on the counter. "Did you spend the night cleaning?"

"Figured I might as well do something useful since I obviously wasn't going to sleep." She took the unmarked whipped cream cheese containers out of the bag and looked at them.

"One's plain and the other has pimento and chives."

"Both sound good." She grabbed small plates from a cabinet and then butter knives from a drawer.

"Look, I know you're an EMT and you've witnessed

traumatic events and learned to cope with the aftermath," Cole said. "But what you're going through is different."

She studied him silently and took a couple sips of her mocha before the timer on the toaster oven rang. She took the bagels out, and both of them smeared on some cream cheese before going over to the dining table to sit down to eat.

Cole took a moment to offer up a quick prayer of gratitude. Emma appeared to do the same. "I just want to say that after my tours in combat zones I had a rough time," he said awkwardly, trying again to bring up what he considered to be the sensitive topic of dealing with one's emotions. "It takes a while to process things. Sometimes you need help. It's good to ask when you do."

"Wow," Emma said after chewing and swallowing a bite of bagel. "That might be the first personal thing you've ever told me."

"Yeah, well." A feeling of self-consciousness crept over him. Maybe he shouldn't have shared that about himself. But the topic was important. He ate a bite of his bagel and then changed the subject. "So what are the plans for today?"

Thanks to their earlier texts, he knew that she hadn't heard from the cops this morning, which seemed to indicate they hadn't made any headway in their search for the attackers. Meanwhile, he was at the end of his rotation for twelve-hour shifts and would be off the work schedule and available to help Emma try to find her brother for the next three days.

"My mom gave me the address for the apartment where Austin's been hanging out with his friends. It's on Marsh Avenue near 10th. She also gave me the phone number for one of the friends but I'd rather not call ahead. I don't know that Austin would leave if he was there and knew we were coming, but I don't want to take the chance."

"Makes sense to me. How's your collarbone feeling?"

"Not that bad. I've been taking the over-the-counter pain pills at regular intervals like the doctor suggested to stay ahead of the pain and so far it's been working."

Her phone chimed and her eyes widened as she reached to grab it from her purse. "Not Austin," she said to Cole after glancing at the screen. She answered the call. "Hi, Shari."

Cole listened as she told Shari that she'd be down in the parking lot within fifteen minutes. "What's going on?" he asked after she disconnected.

"Shari's here to get the library books that are still in my SUV."

Again with the library books.

"After I hand over the books, we might as well go to that apartment and see if Austin is there." She took a sip of her mocha as concern darkened her eyes. "I like to think the kidnappers targeted me because my life is boring and predictable and I'm easy to find. An eighteen-year-old guy like Austin who's kind of untethered and all over the place would be tougher to locate and grab." She took another sip of coffee before tossing the empty cup into a trash can. "I hope I'm not wrong and they've already taken him."

"Let's not get ahead of ourselves." Cole stood and felt the weight of the holstered pistol at his hip, covered by a light jacket. The last thing he wanted to do was shoot anybody. He didn't want to fire his gun at all when he was in town. Bullets could hit something solid and ricochet. Innocent people could get hurt. He'd chosen not to be a cop and he didn't particularly want to function as if he was one. But Emma needed him to use his skills to protect her and keep her safe and alive until this situation with the Los Angeles criminals came to an end.

He drained the last of his coffee and tossed his cup. By then Emma had put on a sweater over her jeans and long sleeve T-shirt. She slung the strap of her shoulder bag over her head. "The coffee and all that sugar helped," she said. "I actually have some energy."

"Enjoy it. We both know you're going to crash in a couple of hours and probably feel worse."

"So I'll let you buy me another extra chocolaty mocha."

The corner of Cole's mouth lifted in a half smile. But then it dropped because he had a point to make and it was serious. "Hold up a minute," he said as she neared the door.

She faced him, hands on her hips. "What?"

"I want to remind you that we need to be extremely vigilant once we step outside that door. No lingering in the parking lot to chat with Shari. Constant attention to our surroundings. Limited amount of time we spend outside of a building or vehicle. We keep a close eye on anybody who comes near us."

"Okay." She dropped her hands from her hips. "I realize you don't have to do this. Thank you."

Cole nodded and then opened the door to check the hallway. Moments later they were downstairs and out in the parking lot where Emma handed over her library books. And, despite the fatigue visible in her eyes and the dark circles beneath them, she actually appeared as if she'd brightened up a little. Cole was happy for her.

Moments later, they were in his truck and on their way to the apartment on Marsh Avenue. Driving through downtown Cedar Lodge, Cole glanced at his rearview and side mirrors as often as was safe. He was gratified to see that Emma was also paying close attention to the other cars and drivers around them.

When they reached their destination, Emma spotted her brother's car. "Looks like it's got a flat, and I know he doesn't have a spare," she said. After they got out of Cole's truck they walked over for a closer view of the listing rattletrap and its deflated tire. Then they changed directions and walked up to the apartment on the ground floor of a two-story building, Cole stepped in front of Emma and knocked on the door. He shielded her body with his, letting his hand hover near his holster. It wasn't so much that he thought Austin and his buddies would be a threat, but that he was concerned the kidnappers might have already tracked Austin to this location. He didn't know how they could have done it, but he'd learned the hard lesson that it never paid to underestimate your adversaries.

A gangly young man with a shaved head and a thin goatee answered the door. A kid trying hard to look like a tough guy was Cole's first impression. Common for so many teenagers. But when the young man's gaze landed on Emma and he smiled, the effect was ruined. Now he looked like a tall, skinny puppy.

"Hey, Emma," the young man said.

"Benny?" she asked after a moment's hesitation.

"Yeah. We met a couple of times."

She nodded. "I remember you."

"So, what's up?" he asked uncertainly.

"I'm looking for Austin. Is he here?"

"Nah. He was here night before last. We stayed up super late playing a game online so he slept over. But then he went home in the morning. His car had a flat so he had to walk. Haven't seen him since."

"Have you *heard* from him?" Cole asked.

"No. I texted him a couple times but never heard back. He hasn't logged on to our favorite gaming site, either." Benny's eyes took on a worried expression. "What's going on?"

Cole was no expert, but he thought the kid's concern and confusion looked genuine.

"I'm worried about my brother," Emma answered. "Someone dangerous came by our parents' house yesterday morning. They've attacked me twice. I think they might be after Austin."

"What?" After staring at her dumbfounded for a few seconds, Benny stepped back inside the apartment and waved them in.

Cole went in first, hand still lingering near his gun in case his reading of Benny was incorrect and this was somehow a trap. Once inside, things appeared fine and Emma followed him in. There were fast-food wrappers and empty soda cups everywhere and the blare from the sounds of an online battle coming from another room.

Benny closed the front door and yelled, "Shawn!"

When there was no response, Benny stalked into the other room and Cole followed him just to be safe. Emma stayed close behind him.

A chubby guy about Benny's age sat in a gaming chair. He gaped at Cole and Emma, then paused the game and took off his headset. "Hey, Emma, what's up?"

Emma might not have remembered much about these guys but they sure remembered her. And honestly, Cole wasn't surprised. She was a striking-looking young woman with dark hair and coffee-colored eyes who typically wore a thoughtful expression on her face, something that Cole had, admittedly, always found appealing.

Benny quickly summarized the situation, and a short conversation made it clear that Shawn hadn't heard from Austin, either. Now both of the roommates looked concerned.

"Where do you think he might be?" Emma asked. "If you had to take a guess."

Benny shrugged and Shawn copied him. "I'm not really sure who he hangs out with besides us these days," Benny added. "He's serious about his job at Burger Bonanza. He's taken on a lot of hours lately. Have you tried there? Otherwise, maybe he's skateboarding at Skate Trek over by Lodgepole Park."

"We saw his car with the flat tire out in the parking lot. How do you think he's getting around town?"

Benny offered another shrug. "His bike or maybe his skateboard? When he left here he said he was going to walk to your parents' house."

Emma's disappointment was obvious by the expression on her face followed by the tone in her voice when she said, "If you see him or hear from him, please tell him to contact me. In fact, I'd like *you* to contact me, too. Give me your phones so I can make sure you have my contact information, and I'll need your numbers, as well."

Cole was impressed by her obvious command of the situation when both guys unlocked their phones and then handed them over so she could add herself to their contacts and then add both of them to her own contact list.

"Let's go," she said to Cole as soon as she was finished and had thanked the young men.

"Sorry you didn't learn anything," Cole said on their way out to his truck. "I know you're disappointed."

"Not just disappointed," she responded in a grim tone. "*Terrified.* If his closest friends haven't heard from him,

I can't help wondering if he's in a horrible situation or if he's even still alive. Who knows what could have happened if the kidnappers went after him and he put up a fight. Maybe they'd rather kill him than let him escape."

Cole simply nodded to acknowledge he'd heard her. Offering reassurances that Austin was likely fine would be dishonest. He walked with his head on a swivel, looking around and staying vigilant. If Austin had already been grabbed, Cole wanted to make sure that Emma wasn't taken next.

"So do you want to try Burger Bonanza next and see if Austin showed up for work yesterday or even today?"

They were seated in Cole's truck, still in the small lot at the apartment complex. Late-morning sunlight shone bright in the blue sky, making the mid-spring day look warmer than it actually was. "Yes." She cleared her throat, tamping down the worry for Austin that was threatening to choke her. *Do not cry.* She wasn't concerned with Cole seeing her break down. He'd seen that already. But she was wary of the possibility that once she started crying, she wouldn't be able to stop for a long time.

"It's getting close to lunchtime," she added. "Maybe he'll have shown up to work a shift." She could hope.

"Let's go." He started up the truck and she turned to him, her attention settling on his strong profile. She used to think of that strong chin and set jaw as hints of politely controlled arrogance. Now it seemed more like confidence and focus. Two qualities she really appreciated. If he wasn't by her side helping her, where would she be now? Even if she'd survived the attacks, she would likely be huddled at home worrying about Austin or dashing around town searching for her brother without much practical knowledge of how to keep herself safe from professional criminals.

Cole started to pull out of the parking slot just as Emma's phone chimed.

"It's Austin!" she called out to Cole, tapping the speaker symbol so he'd be able to hear the conversation. Given the danger to himself he was risking by helping her, it didn't seem right to withhold any information from him. He hit the brakes and put the truck back into Park.

"Where are you?" she demanded as soon as the call connected.

"Hey, sis." Austin's voice came through the phone, sounding amused. "Good to hear your voice, too."

Emma was not in the mood for joking around. "Are you okay?" She glanced toward the apartment building they'd just come from. "Did Benny or Shawn just call you?" Had they been lying to her? Were they actually in contact with Austin? Maybe she and Cole should have checked the closets and under the bed. Maybe he'd actually been hiding in there.

"*Both* of them texted me." Austin sounded more serious now. "They'd messaged and called and stuff yesterday and earlier today and I haven't replied because I've had other things on my mind."

"Is that why you haven't returned my calls?" Emma snapped.

"Kind of. Yeah. Look, I've been staying with a friend and hiking in the woods, thinking, trying to come up with a plan to help clean up this mess I've created and I finally have one."

"This isn't your responsibility." Despite Sergeant Newman's insinuations, Emma was certain her brother hadn't intentionally given away their family's location. And of course he hadn't *sold* the information. It had been her first instinct not to believe he'd done it, and as far as she was concerned the fact that he hadn't disappeared with a large bundle of payoff money never to be heard from again bolstered that opinion. And now here he was trying to come up with a way to solve things.

"Even if you somehow gave away our location back when you were a kid, it still isn't your fault," she continued. "You were a *kid*. Beyond that, were you aware that Mom and Dad were in contact with our grandparents? It's entirely possible that somebody accidentally gave out some information that ultimately led to Walker's thugs finding us." She didn't know exactly how that could have worked. Maybe she had a distant cousin who sold the information. There was no telling. At some point it became impossible to figure out everything.

"I didn't know Mom and Dad broke the rules and stayed connected with the rest of the family," Austin said quietly. "But that doesn't change the fact that I might have messed things up."

"Where exactly have you been staying? Where are you?" Emma demanded for the second time.

"I know the thugs came after you," Austin said, calmly ignoring her question. "I don't want that to happen again. I want to help, so I'm going to draw them out and make it easier for the cops to find them."

Emma's stomach dropped. "No!"

"Watch my social media posts. I'm sure the criminals are looking at my social media as well as yours to try and track us."

Emma was grateful that she didn't spend much time posting on social media, and even then she kept her accounts private. She knew that her brother used the more open public settings because he was young and social and wanted his friends and acquaintances to be able to find him.

"Maybe you could talk to somebody at the police department and let them know to be on the lookout for what I post. I know you have friends there, since cops and the fire department work together so much."

Emma turned to Cole, who was watching her carefully. "Let's go to the police department," she said to him quietly. Fortunately, it wasn't far away.

Cole nodded, drove his truck out of the parking lot and headed in that direction.

"This social media posting is a terrible idea," Emma said to her brother, who was still on the phone.

"No, it's a good idea. I've thought it through and I'll be careful. I'm not a kid anymore, Emma."

Except *he was a kid*. Okay, *legally* he was an adult. He'd graduated high school last June. But he was still her little brother, and a wallop of guilt for not having spent more time with him over the last couple of years hit her hard. "Let's get together and talk about this."

"I'm fine and as I mentioned I have a place to stay," Austin said patiently. "Now, talk to your police friends for me and let them know what's going on. My first post is about to go up. Bye, Emma. Don't worry."

"Wait!"

It was too late, he'd already disconnected. She tried to call him back but he didn't answer.

She looked at the social media site where she knew he tended to be most active. The current post was four days old, well before Royce Walker's criminals had showed up. It was a selfie of her tall, blond-haired brother—who took after their dad—in a shop for outdoor sporting equipment in town, and he was standing beside a display of brightly colored kayaks. Austin did look somewhat grown up, she had to admit. And he was about to put himself in serious danger. She adjusted the settings on her account and her phone so that when Austin made a post she'd get an audible notification.

Meanwhile, Cole had called his cop friend on the truck's hands-free device.

"What's up?" Kris Volker answered.

Cole gave a quick recap of Emma's conversation with her brother.

"Actually, I'm at the station right now. I'll see if the chief and Campbell are available and we can let them know about this."

A short time later, Cole pulled up at the police station and he and Emma hurried inside.

"Thanks for your help," Emma said to Kris as soon as they arrived, trying to keep her cool when her thoughts were frantic.

"Anytime," the cop responded. "The chief is here but Detective Campbell is out of the office. Follow me. The chief is expecting you."

Inside Ellis's office, after a quick greeting, the chief introduced Emma and Cole to the department's public relations and communications officer, Alice Donegal, who was in charge of monitoring the department's social media. She'd already been tapping on her tablet, and she stopped just long enough to offer Cole and Emma a polite greeting and then ask Emma for her brother's name so she could add him to the department's contact list and make sure they received notifications through the department's account.

They'd barely finished their conversation when both

Emma's phone and Officer Donegal's tablet chimed with a notification. Emma tapped her screen and saw a selfie of her brother taken in Lodgepole Park. Water from a tributary of the Meadowlark River was diverted to the park to create a small, decorative stream that flowed through the park with a wooden footbridge over it. Austin had taken the picture of himself on the footbridge, with the lighted signboard on the side of the parks and recreation office visible showing the current date, time and temperature. There was no mistaking that the picture had been taken just moments ago.

Underneath the photo Austin had written, "Got another forty minutes before I have to be back to work at Burger Bonanza. A little cool out here but I don't care. Warm weather will be here soon!"

He'd just told the assailants exactly where to find him.

"I'll head over there now," Volker said.

"I'll have Sanchez and Foster meet up with you." Ellis grabbed a cell phone and called the two additional officers, instructing them on the situation and telling them to meet up with Volker.

"I just forwarded the image to all three officers' phones," Donegal said after the chief disconnected.

Emma stood and turned to Cole. "I want to go to the park, too. If he's still there I want to talk to him."

"Not a good idea," Cole said calmly. "If the kidnappers show up at the park, it could go sideways pretty quickly. They might even change direction and come after you again if they spot you."

"Those creeps might not even be near town right now," Emma argued. Of course she was frightened by the thought of those violent criminals having her in their sights again. But she was more scared that they would get to her brother.

"This could be my one chance to get to Austin before something terrible happens to him. Meanwhile, the thugs might not even see the stupid post."

"Then again, they might."

Frustration had her shaking her head. "But it's such an obvious trap."

"Obvious to you because you know about it. Plenty of people are careless on social media. And since your brother is young, they might assume he's not too bright," Cole argued.

"Don't assume every criminal is some kind of mastermind," the chief interjected. "Plenty of them are far from it."

Emma realized her emotions had gotten the better of her, and she took a deep breath to help center her thoughts.

"Go home," Ellis said. "I'll call you with an update."

"Can't I wait here until you learn something? *Please*."

He sighed. "All right. Help yourselves to coffee in the breakroom and then wait in the lobby. I'll let you know what happens."

Forgoing the coffee, Emma walked with Cole to the lobby where they sat and waited. She prayed while she was there, and repeatedly checked Austin's social media site. Time slowed to a crawl, and she got up to pace and look out the windows numerous times.

Finally, an officer beckoned them from the lobby and escorted them to the chief's office.

"The officers didn't see Austin at the park," Ellis told them. "They took a good look around but he wasn't there. Volker and Sanchez then went to Burger Bonanza at the time he indicated he would return to work and they didn't see him there, either." Emma felt relieved but also disappointed. She'd dared to hope the cops might find Austin and bring him back to the station.

"I have two pieces of information for you from the Burger Bonanza visit," Ellis continued. "His supervisor said he called in this morning to ask for the day off but said he might be in tomorrow."

"What's the other thing?"

"Volker said that when they were inside Burger Bonanza, they noticed a car parked across the street with a couple of guys inside watching the restaurant pretty intently. They appeared to match the description of your kidnappers, so he went outside to get a better look. When the men saw him, the car sped away. Volker got a partial license plate, but I'm sure they've already ditched the vehicle. It was probably stolen."

"So that tells you the thugs were probably there watching for Austin and they're following his posts like he wants them to?"

"I would say so. Which would also tell me that they're still hanging around town looking for you, too. You should go home, make sure your doors and windows are securely locked and get some rest. You look tired, Emma. For good reason. You've been through a lot."

"We can get some food on the way there so you don't have to worry about cooking, unless you want to," Cole added.

They exchanged goodbyes with the chief and headed for the exit. Emma didn't have even the hint of an appetite. She was suddenly so tired she could barely move. She probably should go home and try to get some sleep. It was starting to feel as if she couldn't quite remember what her life had been like back when things were normal. It was starting to look like they might not be normal again for a long time. Maybe not ever.

SEVEN

A piercing shriek yanked Emma from the depths of deep sleep.

For the first few seconds she was disoriented, her heart racing in her chest. The shriek happened again. And then again shortly after that.

By now Emma was sitting up, getting her bearings and she remembered that she'd decided to lay down on the couch in her living room for just a few moments after Cole left. A quick glance toward the dark balcony window, where she'd left the curtains pushed aside, confirmed that she'd slept a lot longer than she'd planned. Instead of just an hour's nap in the afternoon, she'd slept well into the evening.

The shriek sounded again. This time she realized it was coming from the hallway outside her apartment door and that it blared at regular intervals. An alarm. Fire?

She stumbled toward the balcony slider door, threw it open, and was greeted by swirls of smoke and the glow of flames at the ground floor of the building. The structure was designed in craftsman style with lots of exposed wood, and even with everything up to code, a fire could still move quickly.

An eerie-sounding electronic voice recording started

playing in the hallway between the shrieks of the siren. "A fire alarm has been activated. Exit the building immediately. Do not use the elevators."

Emma heard the neighbors' doors opening and closing followed by the sound of footsteps and people talking. A sudden loud pounding on her door made her jump, though given all the other noise it seemed like it shouldn't have. Her nerves on edge, she started toward the door, reaching to unlock and open it, when she remembered to look through the peephole first.

Outside her door she saw the bristly bearded face of her neighbor Gary and his wife, Diana, behind him.

She shook her head. Had she really for a moment thought that the kidnappers had set the building on fire so they could get to her? She needed to find the balance between being vigilant and being paranoid.

"Emma!" Gary shouted just before she unbolted and pulled open the door. "Hey, just wanted to make sure you were okay and heard the alarm. Come on, we need to go!"

"Thanks, yeah, I heard it."

Several other neighbors were in the slightly smoky hallway, some wrapped in blankets or wearing jackets over pajamas as they headed for the stairwell. One of them had stopped to knock on another neighbor's door.

"Right behind you," she said, popping back inside to jam her feet into a pair of boots, shrug on a jacket, pick up her shoulder bag and grab her charging phone.

She followed her neighbors down the stairwell, the smoke getting thicker as they approached the lower floors. By the time she got to the second floor she felt a draft of air and at the ground floor she saw the emergency exit doors propped open. Fire sprinklers had kicked on in the ground floor hallway, as well.

Tenants streamed out the doors and most of them headed toward the building's park-like surroundings. Children were crying, and Emma didn't blame them. It was a scary situation and it was chilly. She pulled her jacket tighter around her body. She heard a fire engine rumbling in the distance, blaring its horn as it drew nearer. Moments later she saw red-and-white flashing lights from several fire trucks heading toward her building. Her friends and coworkers were coming to help.

Emma kept moving away from the building. The last thing she wanted to do was get in the way of firefighters as they hooked hoses to the fire hydrants. She didn't want to get splashed by water, either. Several of her neighbors appeared to have the same idea. She walked across the heavy grass as far as the first cluster of pine trees, which seemed like a reasonable distance.

Facing the building, she watched the emergency response. Her neighbors had drifted in different directions, some of them clustered in small groups, talking and gesturing. Other fellow apartment-dwellers, particularly the ones with children, it appeared, went to sit in their vehicles in the parking lot. Probably so they could start the engine and turn on the heater.

Emma considered getting into her SUV. Standing there cold and alone was not pleasant. At least in her car she could get warm.

"Don't turn around."

Emma felt the tip of a gun pressed against the back of her head. She recognized the voice. It was Bald Guy, the assailant she'd wrestled with on the boat, and he sounded coldly furious.

Despair and regret came over her like a heavy weight, seeming to pull her body downward. Her shoulders slumped instead of tensing in fear. Maybe she'd experienced all the fear she could handle for a while. Perhaps she'd reached the point where it was all too much.

I should have been more careful. I should have spent more time with Austin. I should have known that the bad guys would come after my family one day. I should have been better prepared.

Without moving her head she looked around as best she could, hoping one of her neighbors had seen what had just happened. But that didn't appear to be the case. She and the gunman were in the shadows beneath the thick branches of the group of trees and the exterior lights of the apartment building didn't reach this far.

"Start backing up," Bald Guy demanded.

Emma didn't move. Seemingly all of her neighbors were watching the fire. How ironic it was that her own friends and coworkers were right there fighting that fire. But what did it matter? They didn't know she was in trouble so they couldn't do anything to help her. And Emma had no doubt that letting herself be taken away by the criminals would have horrible consequences.

"I *will* shoot you," the Bald Guy said in an angry tone, his words clipped. Would he actually fire the gun while it was pressed to her skull and kill her right there? He and his partner had the opportunity to kill her before and they hadn't taken it.

Did he figure on shooting to injure her if she didn't cooperate so he could force her away from this spot? And then later he could use the threat of killing her to stop her dad from giving testimony at his boss's trial. If the thugs captured Austin, the power of their threats would be doubled.

"Move, *now!*" The attacker grabbed a handful of the

back of her jacket and pulled her toward him and farther into the darkness.

She took a couple of backward steps and then stumbled over an exposed tree root. Despite her uneven movements, the creep kept a tight hold on her jacket. He pulled her backward again, toward the section of parking lot a few yards away on the other side of the trees. Emma took several more steps and then stumbled again, this time on purpose. She threw her body toward the ground and her shoulder bag slid down her arm. The attacker still held a fistful of her jacket, but he cursed and tilted over and Emma could tell he'd partially lost his footing.

Desperately hoping he wouldn't shoot her, she grabbed the strap of her bag and swung it as hard as she could at the criminal, aiming to knock the gun from his hand. Her plan didn't work. Bald Guy's hand and the threatening gun moved slightly away from her under the force of the impact, but he managed to keep a grip on the weapon. Her bag was still in her grasp. Screaming as loudly as she could, she swung it again and managed to clip him on the side of the face.

He still had a grip on her jacket, though, and she desperately fought to claw her way out of the thing. While struggling to escape the attacker, she caught glimpses of a car with its headlights off idling at the edge of the parking beyond the trees. Ponytail Guy, most likely. And it felt like he was frighteningly close. Once Bald Guy got a good hold on her, it wouldn't take much effort for him to drag her to the getaway car.

The thug was heavier and stronger than she was, but Emma was more limber and could move faster. Twisting at her waist and then arching her back, she didn't make it easy for him to control her. Overwhelmed with frustration and painfully aware that her energy was waning, she screamed again. Though it didn't seem likely that anyone would hear her with all of the sounds from the fire trucks and the firefighters battling the blaze.

In the next moment a bright rectangular light shone in her face. It was followed by a couple more lights and the voice of her neighbor, Gary, yelling, "Get off her!"

The thug cursed and yelled in response, "Back off or I'll kill her!"

Emma couldn't see what was happening; the lights shining in her face were blinding. Apparently, they were blinding to the attacker, too. *Finally*, she felt him let go of her jacket. From the corner of her eye, she could see him holding a hand up to his face as if to block the bright lights shining at him.

"Get a cop over here!" Gary yelled to someone.

Emma hadn't seen a cop car, but she knew it was standard procedure for at least one police unit to respond to a fire call just in case traffic control was needed. An ambulance would be staged nearby, too.

Emma took advantage of the chaos and Bald Guy's disorientation to get to her feet and sprint away in the darkness. She felt the skin crawl on her back as she anticipated a gunshot.

She'd only taken a few steps when Bald Guy actually did fire at her and she dove to the ground. Turning back, she saw that Gary and whoever was with him had doused their cellphone lights so they wouldn't be easy targets.

Emma's eyes adjusted enough to the darkness that she could see the shadowy form of the attacker racing toward the waiting car. He turned and fired two more shots, effectively stopping anyone from pursuing him. Then he hopped in the vehicle and it sped away.

She'd survived, again. *Thank You, Lord.*

Moments later, as she tried to catch her breath and calm her pounding heart, Emma heard the wail of a siren start up. She watched a cop car shoot across the expansive parking lot headed in her direction. Tears of frustration formed in the corners of her eyes as she realized she had nothing new to tell the officer that would help to find the kidnappers. She didn't know what kind of car they'd been driving. She hadn't seen even a small bit of the license plate.

How many times were these thugs going to come after her? As many times as it took to get the job done, apparently. A dark, disquieting thought tugged at the corner of her mind. If she continued to fight back and make herself hard to catch, would the kidnappers respond by putting more effort into finding her brother?

Forty minutes later, Cole knocked impatiently on Emma's apartment door and a cop opened it. Cole looked past the officer at Emma. When he saw the sadness in her eyes and the pine needles in her hair and dirt smudges on her face from her struggle with the criminal loser who'd attacked her, he was overwhelmed with a rush of protectiveness.

He wanted nothing more than to take her in his arms, comfort her and keep her safe. But they were coworkers. If he lost his head and gave in to the rush of emotion, he'd regret his actions eventually. No doubt Emma would feel awkward in the aftermath, too. So what he did instead was step into the apartment, offer a quick nod of acknowledgment to the cop, and then walk calmly toward Emma as the officer closed and bolted the door behind him.

"Hey," Cole said softly, doing his best to maintain the reasonable boundaries of a coworker. *Too late for that*, a quiet internal voice chided him.

"Hey, yourself." Her voice quivered. After a slight hesitation she stepped forward and wrapped her arms around him. Cole blew out a deep breath, one he felt like he'd been holding since his phone rang shortly before 10:00 p.m. and he saw her name on the screen. She told him she'd been attacked again.

The drive from the ranch to her apartment had felt like it took forever as he'd come close to surpassing the legal speed limit on his way there. Outside the apartment building, he'd spotted coworkers from the fire department raking through burned debris on the ground floor to make certain no smoldering ashes remained that could potentially reignite. He'd spoken with one of the firefighters long enough to learn that the fire had been set by piling up a few wooden pallets against the building in the small unenclosed yard of a ground-floor apartment and then setting them on fire. Along with reaching into the walls of the building, the flames had quickly leapt upward to the wooden balcony overhead and that had given the fire fuel to expand.

As Cole raced up the stairs to Emma's apartment, he'd smelled the lingering scent of smoke. His gut had clenched at the realization that the criminals targeting Emma had been willing to set the building on fire in their attempt to get to her.

"I know Rhonda was on shift and covering this part of town tonight," Cole said after their lingering embrace ended and he held her at arm's length to give her a once-over and make certain she was okay. "I didn't see her or the ambulance outside. I'm assuming she determined you were all right and then left?"

"I told her I was fine."

Emma didn't look like she was fine. Cole could see

tears at the corners of her eyes marking a path through the dust on her face. His heart ached at the sight. He was also angry. These thugs *had* to be stopped. He loved being a paramedic, but right now he itched to be a cop so he could help hunt down these criminals.

"What about your collarbone?" Cole asked. "Do you think the injury might have gotten worse after you fought with that loser?"

Emma reached up to touch the injured area. "It doesn't hurt any worse than it did before. I just need to take some more acetaminophen. The pain isn't that bad. I'm just… um…" Her voice broke and she dissolved into tears. "I'm just so *tired* of all of this."

Watching her, Cole felt like he could be on the verge of tears, too. Emma was normally an energetic, confident woman. A great conversationalist who always wanted to talk about something she'd just read. She was solid and reliable and good to have by his side in intense medical emergency situations. Of course she'd been freaked out by the two prior attacks on her. Who wouldn't be? Plus, there was the worry about her parents, specifically her dad, since they could be targets of Royce Walker's criminal gang while they were down in Los Angeles preparing her for dad to testify. And then there was the dangerous behavior of her probably well-intentioned but nevertheless unwise little brother.

And now she'd been awakened by a fire only to be attacked yet again in the nearby park.

She was starting to crumble under the weight of it all, and he knew the feeling only too well. Losing his mom when he was a teenager was a heavy burden that he still carried. Just a few years after that he'd found himself in combat. Seeing his military comrades get gravely or mortally wounded and not being able to do nearly as much as he'd wanted to help them was horrible. Pulling his life together as a young man in the aftermath of that was rough.

Throwing caution aside, Cole let himself give in to impulse and pulled Emma close again. She wrapped her arms around his waist and held on tight, seeming to collect herself as the tears stopped and she took several deep breaths.

Dear Lord, please comfort and strengthen Emma. He knew she was a woman of faith and hoped that she'd been praying and pressing into that faith. Clearly, this was a moment in her life when she truly needed to lean on it.

After they broke off the embrace, the cop who'd been standing by the door walked toward them. "Hi, Cole," he said quietly. "How are you?"

"Kind of have my hands full, Joel." Cole offered the cop, who he knew only slightly, a half smile. "How are you?"

The officer nodded his head toward Emma. "On top of all that's happened, I'm afraid I have to deliver some additional bad news."

"What is it?" Cole asked.

"Royce Walker escaped police custody down in Los Angeles."

For a moment Cole just stared at him, stunned. "How could that happen?"

"Apparently some of his gang members staged an accident on the highway while he was being transported from one facility to another."

"Chief found out shortly before the alarm went out about the fire here," Joel added.

Cole took a deep breath, pushing back against this new added fear for Emma's safety. One thing at a time, if possible, was his rule of thumb whenever he was working in the midst of a chaotic scene. It felt like the last couple of days had been one long chaotic scene. "Back to what happened tonight. Was anybody able to track the criminals who started the fire and grabbed Emma?"

"Not yet." The officer rested his thumbs on his gun belt. "We got a general description of the vehicle from Emma and a decent photo of the attacker taken by Emma's neighbor when he heard her scream and hurried over to help her."

"The guy helped by *taking a picture*?" Cole asked angrily.

"He and some other neighbors turned on their flashlight apps to see what was happening," Emma interjected. "I think that's when he got the picture. But then the shooting started and so they doused their lights, and shortly after that is when I got away from the thug. So ultimately my neighbor did help save my life and I'm grateful."

"I wish the neighbor had tackled the jerk. I suppose having a photo might help identify the kidnapper, but it won't exactly help capture him."

"Maybe not," Joel replied. "But it will help prove he assaulted and attempted to kidnap Emma, which can bring further charges and additional time to his prison sentence after we finally do catch him."

"Obviously these creeps know where you live," Cole said to Emma. "You can't stay here any longer."

"I know," Emma said. She visibly tensed her body for a moment, as if centering herself, and then dropped her shoulders. "It's not your job to look after me, and I'm sure you're already sick of all of this. I know I am." She smiled feebly and brushed aside her dark bangs from in front of her eyes. "I'm going to get a hotel room over in Johnson City. I'll rent a car so the thugs won't recognize me when I drive back and forth between here and there."

A tear escaped from the corner of her eye and she wiped it away. "I *have* to find my brother. I'm scared, but I'm still not going to curl up and hide. Not while Austin is still in town foolishly putting himself in danger because he blames himself for all this trouble."

"Don't be ridiculous." Cole shook his head. "You don't need to go to a town forty miles away. You can stay at the ranch with me and my grandfather. My cousin and her husband live there, too. There's plenty of room."

"I'm not asking you to find me a place to stay."

"I didn't think you were. But I'm offering, nevertheless. I've already mentioned the idea to Grandpa and he's fine with it." Cole cleared his throat. "I was raised by my mom and my grandfather. My dad was not a good person. When my mother left him and moved back to the ranch, my dad showed up armed and belligerent more than once. Grandpa had to deal with him. He's a tough old guy, and the risk of a bit of trouble is not particularly intimidating for him."

Emma stared at him for a moment while biting her bottom lip. "I hate dragging your family into this," she finally said.

Cole offered her a half smile that he hoped was reassuring. "Well, I'm already in it. And given what happened tonight with the fire, I'd say your neighbors have gotten dragged into it as well. *Not by you*. But by the criminals." He shook his head. "Let us help you. We all need to pull together."

"Nobody asked me," Officer Joel said after a few moments passed without Emma responding, "but I think staying with Cole and his family is a good idea and you should take him up on his offer. If the criminals spot you in a rental car and follow you out of town, you'll be a sitting duck on a long, empty stretch of highway."

Emma nodded and then turned to Cole. "Okay, thank you for your generous offer. I accept."

"Good. I'll wait while you pack some clothes."

While Emma got her things together, Joel hung around and chatted with Cole until the transmission came over his radio that the fire and crime scenes were cleared and all responders were returning to their respective stations. The cop left just before Emma came out of her bedroom pulling a suitcase behind her.

"Maybe this will be over soon," she said to Cole as they exited her apartment.

"Yep," Cole said agreeably, hoping that the criminals would be captured without any further violence or danger to Emma. But that didn't seem likely.

EIGHT

"You really do live a long way out of town." Emma looked through the truck window at the dark forest on one side of the road and the moonlit waters of Bear Lake on the other. They were on the back side of the lake, heading up into the mountains. They'd been driving for half an hour.

"It's not exactly convenient," Cole told her. "But it feels like a refuge from the stress of the job and all the people who've moved here over the last few years. It's worth the drive."

Emma glanced over and saw him checking the rearview mirror for probably the tenth time since they'd left town. She checked her side mirror, also on the lookout for anyone who might be following them. So far, all the headlights she'd seen behind them had turned off onto smaller roads leading to residential properties. Still, she couldn't relax. Her clothes smelled of smoke and her collarbone throbbed a little more than she'd let on. She hadn't mentioned it because she didn't want Cole pushing her to get X-rays again. She was sure nothing was broken. It was just the strain of having wrestled with the man who'd pressed a gun to the back of her head.

The memory of that moment flashed into her mind with

an emotional wallop that made her stomach queasy, and she rolled down the window for a gulp of cool, fresh air. *You're okay. Right this minute, everything is fine.* Since the initial attack, she'd had to repeatedly remind herself to stay in the present and not relive the terrifying moments when her life had been threatened. It was either that or curl up into a ball and hide somewhere. She was determined not to do that.

"I think there's a good chance we got out of town without any of the thugs seeing us," Cole said in a reassuring tone as if he understood the anxiety Emma was feeling. "We'll be at the ranch soon."

"You have a lot of crime out here?"

"Nah." He shook his head. "Mainly we just have to watch out for animal predators coming after the livestock."

"What kind of predators?"

"Foxes and coyotes, mostly. Sometimes wolves. Bears now and then. Of course we get hawks coming after our chickens fairly often. We've got to stay vigilant, change up how we respond. Keep guns handy so we can fire warning shots when necessary. Set up traps sometimes."

It really was wilderness out here.

They continued until the lake disappeared from sight and there was only thick forest on either side of the two-lane highway. The topography was more jagged here at the base of a sharp mountain ridge, with the road rising up and then dropping down at regular intervals. Finally Cole slowed almost to a stop and made a sharp turn past a mailbox onto a narrow dirt road.

"We're here," he said.

The driveway up to the house was long. They bumped atop it for several moments, pine branches sometimes brushing against the sides of the truck in the darkness, until they finally crested a small ridge. There, they reached a clearing and Emma could see a sprawling single-story ranch house with warm light shining through a set of big windows at the front of it. They drove closer and she was able to see a wraparound porch. It looked as if this had once been a simple homestead and rooms had been added over the years. The different sections didn't exactly match, but the house looked solid and roomy and homey.

In the moonlight she could see the outlines of a barn and stable with a nearby corral. There were sheds and storage buildings and some other sort of animal enclosures farther away, but she couldn't see them clearly in the dim light. A couple of large pickup trucks were parked in the gravel turnaround driveway, and more vehicles and a horse trailer were parked in a nearby pole shed.

"Looks like everybody's up even though it's the middle of the night," Cole said. "I know they're looking forward to meeting you."

"'Everybody' being your grandpa and your cousin?"

Cole nodded. "My cousin Lauren and her husband, Brent, live here. Grandpa has boarded and trained horses here at the ranch for as long as I can remember, and we all help him with that. Lauren's really into crafts and after Grandpa mentioned that our great-grandparents raised sheep out here when he was a boy, she suggested we start raising sheep for the wool. She has people dye it and spin it into yarn. Turns out there's a market for artisanal craft supplies, and the yarn's been bringing in some pretty good money, so we'll probably expand the operation."

Cole parked the truck and Emma took one more look at her side mirror just to make certain they hadn't been followed before climbing out.

The front door of the house opened, spilling light onto

the floorboards of the wraparound porch. Emma saw the silhouette of a tall, slender and slightly stoop-shouldered man.

"My grandpa," Cole said. "John Webb."

"So this is your paternal grandfather?"

Cole shook his head. "No, he's my mom's dad. My parents got divorced when I was very young. Mom got her original surname back. She had my surname changed to Webb, as well. Apparently my father was willing to go along with the change in return for my mother not pursuing any financial help in raising me."

Emma didn't know what to say. But here was a reminder that having a challenging family life wasn't unique to her. Yeah, they had to go into a witness protection program, but there were worse things that could happen.

Cole grabbed Emma's suitcase and they headed for the house.

"Come on in," the older man urged as they drew closer. "It's chilly out there."

Emma walked past Cole's grandpa, who appeared to be in his mid- or late-seventies. The older gentleman still retained chiseled facial features similar to his grandson, but he had brown eyes instead of blue and a head of thick silver hair.

"Welcome," he said after he closed the door. "I'm John, but feel free to call me Grandpa. Everyone does."

Emma smiled and shook his outstretched hand. "Pleased to meet you."

A couple of large dogs made their way to the shallow foyer. "This here's Liza," Grandpa said, patting a mellow black lab with a graying muzzle. "And that's Misty," he added, indicating a younger-looking German shepherd with a furiously wagging tail.

"We live here, too," a young dark-haired woman in sweatpants and a long-sleeve T-shirt said with a laugh. "Hi, I'm Lauren, Cole's cousin." She took hold of the hand of the man standing beside her, a stocky guy with a round face and wavy dark-blond hair. "This is my husband, Brent."

"Nice to meet you," Brent said with a smile.

Emma nodded. "Good to meet you, too," she added while scratching the head of the black lab.

Both Lauren and Brent had errant locks of hair sticking out at odd angles, and Brent had a button obviously fastened through the wrong buttonhole on his shirt. Emma was painfully aware that she'd gotten these people out of bed late at night when they likely were used to getting up very early in the morning. Feeling suddenly awkward and burdensome, Emma leaned to pet the German shepherd as it chomped on a chew toy.

"Thank you all so much for letting me stay here," Emma said after straightening. "I don't plan to be here long."

"You stay as long as you need to," Grandpa said in a warm growl. "Decent people shouldn't have to seek refuge from danger, but the world is what it is. It's a blessing for us to do what we can to help." He pulled out a drawer from a small table beside an easy chair and gestured at the handgun that was inside. "Given all that's happened to you lately, I'm determined to stay prepared for trouble."

Touched by the man's gruff kindness, Emma blinked back tears and glanced around the front room. There was a large fireplace, with no fire burning at the moment, understandably. The floor was made of wooden planks, with colorful thick rugs thrown atop it. The sofa and chairs were sturdy and upholstered in leather, with knitted throws folded and lying along the backs of them.

She figured the beautiful yarn used to make them was a product of the family business.

Ahead of her and to the right, hallways led to other rooms. To the left, she could see a large, heavy wooden dining table and part of a kitchen.

"Let me get you something to eat," Grandpa said. "Or I can put on a pot of coffee."

Emma quickly shook her head. "Oh, no. Thank you." These people were already doing so much for her.

"I made a couple of apple pies day before yesterday," Brent said. "Surprisingly, there's still some left." He shot Cole a meaningful look.

"I'd think you would take it as a compliment when you bake things and people want to eat them," Cole said unapologetically.

Lauren stepped forward and reached for the handle on Emma's luggage. "Would you like to go to your room and get some rest?"

"I'd love to."

"The dogs will bark if anyone comes around the house," Cole said quietly.

Emma gave him a grateful nod. "Thank you, for everything." The words seemed so small in relation to all the man had done for her. But she didn't know what else to say. "Good night," she said to Grandpa and Brent. Lauren had already started down the hallway, rolling Emma's suitcase behind her.

They walked past an office, a bathroom and a den with more thickly padded furniture and knitted throws and a big TV on the wall.

"Did you knit the throw blankets?" Emma asked.

"Yes," Lauren said over her shoulder. "I knit in the winter when things slow down a little and I have the time. I do a little spinning, too, though most of that I contract out. There are a lot of people around here learning or trying to preserve some of the old ways of doing things. It's work, but it's also rewarding. And there are people who are willing to pay for good-quality hand-spun yarn, which obviously helps. We aren't a big ranch, but we're doing our best to keep things going and trying to expand little by little."

Emma appreciated the friendly chatter as they walked. On the drive over she'd started to feel as if her life was contracting into a pinpoint of intense anxiety and fear. She needed a reminder of what it was like to have her thoughts dwell on things other than the security of her family and her own battle to stay safe.

"Here's the guest room," Lauren said, flicking on a light switch. There was a large window on one wall, and Emma immediately stepped toward it to pull the curtains closed so that she wouldn't be an easy target for someone outside. So much for trying to get her thoughts away from danger.

"Sorry," Lauren said quietly. "I should have thought of that."

Emma offered her a smile and then said, "It's a beautiful room." A handmade quilt covered the double bed. A rocking chair sat in one corner with a tabby cat curled up on the cushion.

"Louie, come on." Lauren started toward the rocking chair. The cat lifted his head, opened his eyes and then slowly blinked a couple of times.

"Don't take him out of here on my account," Emma said. "I love cats and I'd like the company. I'll leave the door open when I go to bed so he can go out if he wants to."

"You'd better be sure. There's a good chance he'll climb in bed with you. Louie is a cuddler."

"I'm sure."

Lauren scratched the cat under the chin. "You be good." Then she gestured toward a narrow, partially open door inside the bedroom. "This room has its own bath with a shower. Towels are in the cabinet. There's body wash and shampoo in there."

The hospitality being offered was beyond anything Emma had expected, and it was a bit overwhelming.

"I'll go so you can get some rest," Lauren said, walking toward the hallway. "If you need anything, let us know. Good night."

"Good night." Emma sat down on the bed as Lauren closed the door behind her.

Louie got up and stretched and then jumped on the bed. Emma needed to go to sleep soon. Morning was not far away and she had to resume her attempts to find Austin. His decision to taunt the criminals and draw them out so the cops could capture them was such a terrible, misguided idea. One that could get him killed.

She should have kept a closer eye on him over the last couple of years. If she had, she would have known him better and it might have been easier to predict his behavior and find him.

Emma lay on the bed, fully clothed, resting her head on the pillow and staring up at the ceiling. Changing into pajamas and getting under the covers would make her feel too vulnerable. She needed to be ready to run at a moment's notice because anything could happen at any time. The most she could bring herself to do was kick off her shoes so they wouldn't damage the quilt.

Louie curled up beside her.

Emma had done her best to appear pulled together and calm in front of Cole and his family. But the truth was, she was still emotionally processing all of the events of the night. How many attacks could she survive? As many as she had to was the only reasonable answer. And it wasn't enough for her just to survive. She needed to take whatever risks were necessary to protect her family.

"You want to keep repairing that gate or should we just build a new one?" Cole walked up to his grandfather the next morning where John was working on strengthening a few sections of fencing at the corral. Cole carried his own cup of coffee plus one for the older man. He knew his grandpa would need a little extra caffeine after having his sleep interrupted last night.

John straightened and stretched his back before reaching for the mug. "I got the gate fixed so that it will hold for a while, but we should probably go ahead and build a new one." He took a long, lingering sip of coffee.

Cole glanced up at the clear blue sky overhead. It was still dusky-looking on the horizon and still early for most people, but not particularly early for ranch life. Even though Cole had his paramedic job with its own hours, he still found it hard to sleep in on workdays when he wasn't on the schedule at the fire station. The rhythm of getting up and getting things done as soon as there was daylight had settled into his blood at an early age and wouldn't let go.

"Is Emma awake yet?" Grandpa asked.

"Apparently she wasn't as of a few minutes ago. I didn't see her in the kitchen, and I know if she smelled coffee she'd come and get some." Nobody in his family drank the flavored coffee creamers that Emma was so fond of. The best he'd been able to do was put a bag of sugar on the counter alongside a bottle of chocolate syrup. She had to know there was milk and cream in the fridge, and a determined woman like her was bound to figure out a way to make it all work to her liking.

"So, these men that are after her, you think they might target you now, too?" Grandpa asked. "At this point they must have figured out you're helping her."

Cole shrugged. Grandpa obviously knew the answer by the way he framed the question. "I'll be careful," he said.

"See that you are."

A clanging sound came from the stables, and moments later Lauren walked out carrying a metal bucket in each hand. She grabbed a hose, rinsed the buckets and filled them with fresh water and then took them back inside. Brent led a trio of horses out of the stables and into a nearby fenced meadow.

"It's looking good out here," Cole said. When he'd returned to Cedar Lodge from his stint in the Navy, the ranch had fallen into disrepair. The horses his grandfather boarded were well taken care of, but other buildings on the property were close to tumbling down. Grandpa had been out here by himself, doing the best he could, but it had looked like the family ranch might end with him. Cole hadn't been willing to let that happen. He was grateful that Lauren and Brent had likewise seen the value of their heritage, and they'd moved to the ranch to help out. It had been slow going and expensive getting things back on track, but the investment of time and money was paying off.

Atop a nearby grassy hill, a couple of sheep bleated. Liza and Misty trotted among them, keeping an eye on things. While not trained to herd sheep, both dogs had a natural protective instinct and strong territorial drive that meant they'd bark a warning and even launch an attack if they smelled or saw animal predators nearby.

Grandpa took another sip of coffee. "You know, when I mentioned that I was looking forward to you bringing a girl home, I didn't mean like this. A woman with criminals chasing after her." The older man laughed quietly at his own edgy joke and then turned to his grandson. "But I should have known this was how it would be." His expression became more thoughtful. "You've always wanted to help people or heal them, like your mom. It's a good instinct to have."

"Emma doesn't need me to help or heal her." Cole glanced at the dogs and then back at his grandfather. "I mean, she needs our help to give her a place to stay where the thugs can't find her. But she, personally, is a strong woman who doesn't need me to fix her in any way."

It was true. And the realization struck Cole that this was something different for him. He'd dated four very nice women over the last few years, but in each case they'd been facing a tough situation in their personal life and they'd needed him to lean on until things got better. And then they'd broken up because that kind of connection by itself just wasn't enough to build a long-term relationship.

It was just now dawning on Cole that he'd chosen those kinds of situations, even if unconsciously. And now with Emma, well, things were different. And confusing. Because the more he was around her, the more he realized he just flat-out liked her. Those countless conversations they'd had while working together had formed a foundation. She was smart and funny and strong. A woman he felt he could lean on if he had to. Even after finding out she wasn't exactly who she said she was. And that was a situation he'd been wary of since he was an adolescent and his mother had started telling him the truth about his father. How he had been a con man who exuded charm and trustworthiness that just wasn't real.

Cole understood why Emma hadn't been forthcoming about her true identity. He'd been put off at first, and suspicious. But after learning her family was in a witness protection program, he realized how reasonable it had been to do that.

"Emma seems like a nice woman." John took another sip of coffee.

"She's a coworker," Cole said, mostly to remind himself. Because this new understanding of whatever relationship they had made him realize things were in danger of getting out of control between the two of them and he couldn't allow that. Cedar Lodge was a small town. They both worked for the fire department. If their relationship turned romantic, that could potentially put both their livelihoods in danger if things didn't work out. Or even if things did work out, it could be a problem working together.

"I brought her here because she needed a safe place to stay," Cole emphasized again. "That's the only reason."

His grandfather made a scoffing sound. "The both of you work in the fire department right next to the police department where you have lots of friends. I'm glad she's here, don't get me wrong, but you can't convince me there wasn't anybody else who would have helped her out if you hadn't."

Cole turned to his grandfather and lifted an eyebrow. "You taking up a new career giving romantic advice this late in life?"

John drew himself up. "I won over your grandmother. The kindest, smartest, most beautiful woman in the state of Montana agreed to marry me. So yeah, I'd say I am indeed qualified to give romantic advice."

"You make a good point."

The kitchen door of the house opened and Emma walked out. Glancing toward the corral, she spotted Cole and his grandfather. She started in their direction, coffee mug in one hand and phone in the other.

She exchanged greetings with both men before gesturing to Cole with her phone. "I've been looking for a new post from Austin, but I haven't seen one yet."

"Maybe he thought about it and realized his plan wasn't so smart." Cole quickly summarized Austin's recent activities to his grandfather, who shook his head in response.

Emma sighed heavily. "I'd like to believe my brother had a sudden burst of good sense, but I can't count on it."

Cole noted the dark circles still under her eyes. "How'd you sleep?"

She shrugged. "I was awake for a while, thinking, but I finally drifted off. Right now I've got some energy, but I don't know how long it will last. So we need to get moving."

"Okay," Cole said cautiously. "Where do you want to go?"

"Burger Bonanza. They serve breakfast sandwiches so they'll be open. I want to see if Austin is reckless enough to show up for work even after mentioning it in his social media post. He's got to need money so he might risk it. If not, well, maybe we can learn something useful from one of the other employees."

"All right." His first choice would have been to keep her at the ranch and away from danger, but it wasn't his decision to make. The kidnappers were determined to get to her. Cole would do his best to stand in their way.

NINE

"It's not only your brother who could put himself in danger by coming here," Cole said to Emma as he pulled into a parking space at Burger Bonanza. "If the kidnappers are watching this place in hopes of finding your brother, they'll obviously see and recognize you, too." He made sure to keep his tone mild because it wasn't his intention to imply she didn't know better. What he was hoping for was that she'd change her mind and let him drive her back to the ranch.

"If you have a better idea on how to find Austin, I'm listening." She turned to him.

Cole's gaze settled on her face for a moment. Her coffee-colored eyes held an expression of trust that made his heart feel like it was expanding. His breath tightened a little bit and he felt a pleasant fluttering his stomach. *Butterflies? Seriously?*

He really was falling for his work partner, and he was determined not to allow those emotions free rein for so many reasons. Not least of which was, at the moment, he needed to keep a sharp eye on their surroundings. He forced himself to break his gaze away and have a look around.

Turning back to her, he cleared his throat. "The only thing I can think of to do is go back to the apartment and talk to his buddies again. Get names and contact info for some of the other people in Austin's social circle. Maybe we can figure out which friend is helping him. While we're at it, we could look to see if Austin's car is still out front. If not, it would suggest he came by to fix the flat tire. Seems likely that before he drove away he'd take a minute to visit with Benny and Shawn."

Emma lifted her eyebrows, pursing her lips as she offered an approving nod. "I knew you'd find a way to make yourself useful."

Cole smiled in return. He really had enjoyed working with her the last couple of years. Too bad he hadn't truly appreciated that until now.

They got out of the truck and headed for the restaurant. Like so many establishments in Cedar Lodge, Burger Bonanza had started out small and expanded more recently. The original walk-up window with nearby picnic tables was available in warm weather; otherwise, there was a drive-through and an enclosed dining area.

"Let me do the talking," Emma said as they stepped inside and headed toward the order counter. "For one thing, no one's likely to find me intimidating."

Cole flashed her a half smile. "They would if they knew you." But he realized what she meant. She was a petite woman and not physically imposing.

She drew herself up, a grin playing across her lips. "Thanks for the compliment."

By the time they approached the counter, her expression had sobered. The momentary lightheartedness was gone. Once again, she appeared to have the weight of the world on her shoulders. And right now Cole wanted nothing more than to ease that burden for her.

There were a handful of customers in the dining area

but it wasn't especially busy. Emma walked directly up to a young woman who looked to be in her early twenties behind the counter. She wore a denim shirt with the name Leanne embroidered on it.

"Hi, Leanne," Emma said. "My brother Austin works here and I need to speak with him for a minute."

"Austin?" Leanne glanced over her shoulder toward a pass-through into the kitchen area. "I haven't seen him. Are you sure he's working today?"

"Actually, I'm not. Has he been at work for the last few days?"

"I don't know. I generally work store opening, breakfast service and lunch prep, so I just see him now and then when he comes in early to help cover for the lunch rush."

"Is there a manager on duty I could talk to?"

"Sure."

Leanne stepped out of sight and moments later returned with a woman who appeared maybe a decade older than her following behind. She also wore a denim shirt with the name Wendy, Assistant Manager, embroidered. "How can I help you?" Wendy asked politely.

Leanne explained that Emma was here to ask about her brother.

"Austin is such a good worker and a nice young man," Wendy said. "He shows up on time and does a good job. Please don't tell me he's in some kind of trouble."

"He's not in trouble." Emma shook her head. And then she appeared to reconsider her words. "Not in trouble in the sense that he did something wrong. But some dangerous people have a grudge against him."

The front door opened and both Emma and Cole quickly turned. A couple of moms each with a small child. Not the kidnappers. Cole let out the breath he hadn't even realized he was holding. He and Emma turned back to the counter as the women and children came up behind them.

Wendy nodded toward a door at the end of the counter and then walked down and opened it, stepping into the lobby to speak more privately. "Austin called out for the day yesterday. Didn't claim he was sick, just said he couldn't come in. He did the same thing last night, only he sent a message instead of actually calling, saying he wouldn't be in to work today, either."

"Maybe some of his other coworkers know where he's been the last couple of days?" Emma said hopefully. "Perhaps we could ask them if they know anything."

Wendy looked at her for a moment. "Wait here." She went back through the door into the work and kitchen area.

"Maybe we'll get a good lead," Emma said.

Uncertain whether it would be kinder to encourage that hope or to downplay it, Cole ultimately said nothing. Seeing the spark of happy anticipation in her eyes made his heart feel like it was balancing on the edge of a precipice. If she ended up painfully disappointed, he would feel her hurt, too.

Wendy returned to the lobby. "A couple of people said they see him in Lodgepole Park now and then. And sometimes riding his skateboard nearby at Skate Trek."

Cole watched Emma's shoulders sag with disappointment and he shared the feeling.

"If I leave you my contact info, can you ask your other employees if they know anything about Austin's whereabouts when they show up for work?"

After a moment's consideration Wendy shook her head. "I don't know exactly what's going on and I don't think I should involve myself or our employees. If you want to come back just to see if he's here, that's fine. But when it comes to asking all the other employees about Austin, well, I need to ask my manager what he thinks before I do that. I don't want to step over some HR privacy boundary."

"I understand." Eyes downcast, Emma nodded. "Thank you."

Wendy went back to work and Emma stood for a moment before turning to Cole. The combination of toughness and vulnerability he saw in her eyes drew him to her. But right now she seemed so focused on what she was doing, so determined to get the job done, that reaching out with a comforting touch or hug didn't seem like the right thing to do. So instead, he asked her if she wanted a coffee while they were there. Burger Bonanza might emphasize their chili dogs and onion rings, but like any self-respecting food and beverage business in northern Montana, they offered an array of hot and cold coffee drinks.

"Yes, please," she said in response to his offer. "Double mocha with a marshmallow syrup."

Cole cringed and didn't hide it. "That's a lot of sugar."

"I know," Emma said. "That's the point. Right now I need all the caffeine and sugar-fueled energy I can get."

"You're going to sugar crash hard this afternoon."

"Not if I drink another one."

Cole sighed.

Emma glanced over her shoulder at the booths. "I'm going to go sit down."

"Probably be better if we stay together."

"Oh, right."

The windows were lightly tinted, and each of them had at least one cardboard sign attached to it advertising an item or food combo on special so it probably wouldn't be easy for anyone outside to spot them. If the kidnappers were watching the restaurant, they'd already know that

Cole and Emma were there. An attack would more likely come when they walked outside. Still, staying close together struck Cole as a good idea.

They ordered their coffees and the drinks were ready just as Emma's phone chimed.

She looked at the screen. "It's Sergeant Newman, the federal witness protection liaison. I wonder what he wants."

Cole picked up both coffees so Emma could take the call. He carried them toward a corner booth away from the windows where there were no other customers seated nearby.

Emma put the call on Speaker. "Hello."

"Hey, Emma," the familiar voice came through. "Thought I'd call to see how you're holding up."

Emma looked at Cole before answering, a guarded expression on her face. "I'm doing okay," she said cautiously. "How are you?"

"Keeping busy. So, I was wondering, have you seen your brother? I'm concerned about him."

"Why exactly are you concerned about him?"

"To be blunt, I'm worried that the criminals from Royce Walker's gang who've been coming after you will come after him, too." He cleared his throat, "Look, if Austin sold them information on how to find your dad, but your dad was whisked away before the thugs could get to him, they're going to be angry. At the least, they'll want any money they paid out to him returned. Worst-case scenario, they might hurt him."

Cole watched an expression of horror cross Emma's face. He reached across the table to lightly grasp her forearm. Just to let her know he was there with her. To remind her that he had her back. Maybe to somehow give her added strength because she was going through so much.

"Are you there?" Newman asked after Emma didn't respond right away.

"Yes." Emma appeared to struggle to speak as she looked down at her phone. "I'm here."

Cole loosened his grip on her forearm and reached up to rest his hand on her shoulder. He didn't have any siblings, but he had three friends who were like brothers. He had cousins like Lauren that he was close with. He had at least an inkling of what Emma was feeling right now and it was awful.

Emma lifted her gaze to look at Cole. There were tears in the corners of her eyes and her face was red. To Cole's surprise, instead of looking scared or hopeless now, she looked angry. "Thank you for the warning about the danger my brother is facing." She directed the words, in a roughened voice, toward her phone.

"Emma, you haven't answered my question," Newman responded with a hint of reprimand. "Have you seen Austin? Do you know where he is?"

Cole wasn't wild about the deputy's tone. It was tempting to say as much, but this was Emma's battle and she was handling it just fine without Cole butting in.

"The answer to both of your questions is 'no,'" Emma said to Newman. "I haven't seen Austin, I don't know where he is, and I will tell you right now that he *did not* betray our parents. If anybody in my family said or posted something that helped the vicious criminal gang find us here in Cedar Lodge, it was done by accident. Stop trying to pin the blame for all of the horrible things that are happening on my brother."

After wiping the angry tears from her eyes, she added, "I have to go. Goodbye." Then she disconnected the call.

Cole took his hand from her shoulder, sat back and took

a sip of his coffee. If she wanted to talk, she would. If she wanted to sit together in silence while she collected her thoughts, he was fine with that, too. He glanced out the windows to check the parking lot, but he didn't see anything out of the ordinary. Emma took several sips of her sugary coffee. A handful of customers had come into the restaurant while they were on the call with Sergeant Newman. None of them looked suspicious to Cole.

Emma sniffed loudly. She dug a tissue out of her purse to wipe her eyes and then her nose. "At first there was a tiny little part of me that suspected Austin might have intentionally done something impulsive and stupid to give away our family's location." She shook her head. "Now I feel so bad for having doubted him." New tears started to fall. "I feel so bad for not having made more of an effort to hang out with him the last couple of years."

She'd mentioned that same regret before, and Cole was saddened to see that it still had such a tight hold on her.

Her phone chimed. "Now, what?" she grumbled, tapping the screen.

Cole looked down and saw a notification from the social media platform where Austin had previously posted his location to try to draw out the bad guys.

"Austin's put up a new post," Emma said, her voice barely more than a whisper. "It's a picture of him at Lodgepole Park. Looks like it's on the edge of the park near the woods."

Cole was looking at the picture upside down. Austin had a bag of chips and a silver can of soda in his free hand while he snapped a selfie with the other.

"Beautiful spot to enjoy the morning near Cub Inlet before I have to go to work in an hour," Emma said, reading the post. "So fortunate to live in Cedar Lodge."

"Let's head to the police station," Cole said. Maybe the cops would find Austin before it was too late.

They got up and left the restaurant, with Cole cautiously scanning the parking lot for signs of danger before they headed for his truck. Sergeant Newman's call and Austin's post were both fresh reminders of the danger that surrounded Emma. And Cole, too, if he got caught in the crossfire.

Once again, the wait at the police station was excruciating. Chief Ellis had promised an update after his officers went to Lodgepole Park to search for Austin. Emma sat in the lobby beside Cole, her hands clasped tightly together, feeling like her stomach was being clamped in a vise. "I should have gone to the park," she finally said. "Maybe if Austin could see me, he'd talk with me and I could convince him how foolish this is." She'd phoned him many times since their last conversation, but he never picked up the call.

"I don't want to be harsh," Cole said, "but you intentionally putting yourself where the kidnappers might show up is not a great idea, either."

"I know," Emma muttered. She wasn't offended by his comment, and she knew he was right. "It just feels crummy waiting around and not doing anything."

"I get it. We both work as first responders, and we both have the drive to do something to help. It's frustrating when the most beneficial thing you can do is stay out of the way."

Terrible images popped into Emma's mind of things that could be happening at this moment. Like the thugs violently attacking Austin. Killing him, even. She couldn't seem to stop the horrifying thoughts no matter how badly she wanted to. She rubbed her fingertips against her temples, trying to ease the pounding tension headache that had a tight hold on her. She'd forgotten to take the acetaminophen tablets this morning and now her collarbone was throbbing. Probably because her whole body was pulled tight with nerves.

"Kris is a good cop," Cole said. "If there's something that needs to be done, he and his team will take care of it."

"I know."

When Emma and Cole arrived at the police department shortly after leaving Burger Bonanza, they'd learned Kris Volker was on duty. Officer Donegal had already alerted the Chief to Austin's post, and Kris had been called into Ellis's office. Kris, along with three other officers, had been directed to change into civilian clothes so they would blend in and then head to the park to search for Austin while keeping an eye out for the thugs.

Now, an hour later, Emma checked her phone yet again, thinking maybe her brother would put up something new on his social media account. Maybe he'd even call or text her to let her know the cops had shown up and the assailants had been captured.

But there was no new communication from him.

Dear Lord, please protect Austin.

She took a sip of the marshmallow mocha she'd brought with her from Burger Bonanza. It had gone cold, but it was still sugary and full of caffeine and that's what she needed.

Finally, the door to the lobby from the patrol room opened and Kris Volker, dressed in jeans and a flannel shirt instead of his usual police uniform, stuck his head out. "Come on back."

"Is he with you?" Emma asked, bounding to her feet and following him through the door. "Did you find Austin?"

Kris stopped and looked at her. "No, I'm sorry but we didn't." He turned and briskly led the way past rows of desks and toward the chief's glass-walled office.

Emma stood for a moment, doing her best to collect her colliding emotions of disappointment and despair, and then she began to follow the cop at a slower pace. Her footsteps felt heavy and her heart sank in her chest.

"Have a seat," Ellis said to Cole and Emma when they reached his office. Then he turned to Kris. "Go ahead and tell them what you told me."

Kris cleared his throat. "When the other officers and I got to the park, we fanned out and individually headed for the spot Austin indicated in his post."

"Was he there?" Emma interjected impatiently. "Did you at least see him?"

"A flash of movement a few yards away caught my eye. I thought maybe it was a reflection off the can your brother was holding in the picture, so I headed in that direction. By that time one of the other officers had caught up with me. The person I spotted, or *think* I spotted, vanished in the forest and we couldn't catch up with them." Kris shrugged. "Might have been Austin. Might have been one or both of the kidnappers. Or it might have been someone completely different."

"Maybe it was an animal," Cole said quietly. "Light filtering down through tree branches to the forest floor can play tricks with your eyes."

"That's right," Chief Ellis agreed. "Clearly Austin had the simplistic idea that the bad guys would brazenly show up to the spot that he'd posted about and it would be easy for us to grab them. Apparently theses crooks are more sophisticated than that." Ellis cleared his throat. "Detective Campbell has a team of investigators working hard to find the thugs who've targeted you. They're very busy interviewing witnesses, visiting locations to look for security video and then actually watching that video. That takes a lot of time. I don't have the staff available right now to keep responding to your brother's posts. In fact, I believe responding to your brother's postings might encourage him to keep going with that plan and that's not what we want to do."

"So you're no longer going to look for him and make sure he's okay when he posts those selfies and announces where he is and how long he's going to be there?" Emma demanded, panic clawing up her throat. "He's doing that to try and help you catch the criminals." What would she do now? Head for the locations herself if Austin kept posting them?

"Call Austin, and if he doesn't answer leave him a message summarizing what I just said," the chief responded calmly. "Let him know we tried to work with his plan and it's failed both times. Despite what you might think, as his older sister you probably have more sway over what he decides to do than you realize. Tell him it's time to knock this off. We don't have the resources to waste on something that's not going to work. We need to find these thugs before they kill somebody." He gave Emma a lingering look, as if to emphasize the danger that had been stalking her. "Tell him he's not in trouble, but we'd like to talk with him. At the very least, he should talk with you."

"Maybe he'd listen to your parents if you got them to relay the message," Cole suggested.

Emma shook her head. "I don't know how much I want to tell them about this." She'd spoken to them earlier this morning, but she'd kept her communication with them about the dangers she and Austin faced at a minimum. Her mom and dad already had enough to worry about. As a result of Royce Walker's escape, his murder trial was back on hold again, of course. But the US Marshals were confident they would find him quickly, so the prosecutor's office had asked Emma's parents to remain in Los Angeles for at least a week.

It felt to Emma like things kept going from bad to worse. Her parents were stuck in Royce Walker's home territory. Even with professionals protecting her mom and dad, there was always the possibility that vicious criminals could get past the guards. Beyond that was the fact that their lives had been completely disrupted and there was no telling how long that would last. Both of her parents worked from home, but that didn't mean they could walk away from work obligations without eventually facing financial repercussions. It was all a big mess, and as much as she wanted to fix it, she couldn't.

Cole reached for her hand and squeezed it. "We'll get through this."

She nodded. "Yes, we will." Faith and prayer had held her together so far. But Cole and his caring demeanor had helped, too. Very much.

Emma took a deep breath and got to her feet. Cole stood alongside her. "I'll try again to get Austin to stop what he's doing with these posts," she said to the chief.

"Might be best if you just hung out at the Webb family ranch where you'll be safe," Ellis replied. "Maybe you could stay out of town and let us find your brother and the kidnappers."

Emma simply nodded in response. While she didn't want to cause problems for the police, she also didn't want to give assurances she didn't intend to keep. She and Cole exchanged their goodbyes with Kris and the chief, and then they headed for the exit.

Emma understood the chief's frustration with her brother. She was frustrated and annoyed, too. But that didn't mean she would stop trying to find him before it was too late and he got himself killed.

TEN

"I don't want you to miss any more work because of me," Emma said to Cole. They'd just left the police station and were now approaching the fire station a short distance down the road. "In fact, I should apologize for dragging you into all of this," she continued. "It isn't fair that your whole life is being disrupted by my problems."

In the wake of the initial attack on Emma, both the police chief and her boss at the library had agreed to an open-ended leave of absence until her situation could be resolved. Just now, Cole had said he wanted to talk to the chief about taking more time off. As it stood, Cole was scheduled to report back to work tomorrow.

"If I didn't want to get involved, I wouldn't," Cole said as they walked through an open roll-up door into one of the cavernous fire engine bays. "Besides, if something happened to you, I could end up with a work partner who never cracked a book and had nothing interesting to talk about on slow nights."

Emma let a smile play across her lips. His teasing tone lightened her mood a little despite the dangerous threats swirling around her.

"I'll sit in the crew room while you talk to the chief," Emma said. Cole nodded and walked toward the administrative offices while Emma threaded her way between an engine and ladder truck parked in the bay and headed for the breakroom. A team of firefighters inventorying the ladder truck greeted her, and they spoke for a few minutes. Through the open doors at the back of the station, she could see another team rolling up a recently used fire hose and readying it to be packed back onto an engine.

When she reached the breakroom, she dropped down onto a couch and took out her phone to call her parents. She tapped the screen for her mom's number and the call rolled to voicemail. She left a message: "I hope you and Dad are being well-protected. Please call Austin and tell him the cops want him to stay completely off social media. Also, tell him to contact me. Thanks. Love you."

Her next call was to Austin. "Call me. *Now.* The social media posts obviously haven't worked and the cops are not going to respond to them by showing up at the location you post anymore. Placing me in the position of having to go look for you is exposing me to added danger and I don't appreciate that." She exhaled a small sigh. "Look, I'm not mad at you," she said in a softer tone. "I just want you to be okay. And I genuinely want to see you and talk to you. So call me. Bye."

What if the thugs had already gotten to him? What if that flash of movement Kris had thought he'd seen was real and it was the kidnappers taking her brother away? They could be dragging him down to their home turf in California by now. And what if they offered to set Austin free if their dad traded himself in return for the freedom of his son? It would be just like Dad to do that.

Lord, I know our times are in Your hands. I pray for Your protection and comfort for all of us. I pray for guidance and wisdom. I pray for strengthened faith.

The prayer helped to ground her. She was still afraid, still uncertain and still frustrated with her brother's foolish behavior. But in spite of that, she now felt a sense of being upheld. She remembered that she was not on her own in all of this. Her concerns remained, but the spiraling, frantic energy of her thoughts began to settle down.

The door to the crew room opened and Cole walked in. "You didn't brew a fresh pot of coffee while you were here? *Seriously?* How are you going to get that follow-up dose of caffeine and sugar to keep you going?"

Emma turned to him and rolled her eyes. "Funny." But then she smiled and added, "So what's your work schedule?"

Cole walked around and sat beside her on the couch. "Rhonda is happy to pick up extra shifts since her daughter is a high school senior this year, and we know how expensive that can be. County Fire and Rescue is willing to stage a paramedic and EMT crew at our station house if it's needed. This is with the understanding that if your situation drags on for more than another three or four days, it will all have to be renegotiated. Maybe you'd be willing to spend more time hanging around at the ranch while I work, if need be. And then I could take time off of work to come to town with you when you have a specific lead to follow. Something along those lines."

"I don't know about just *hanging around* at the ranch," Emma said. "I can help out. I'm sure I could wrangle chickens or take the goats for a walk or something."

Cole laughed. "That would be helpful. Maybe you could frolic with the sheep, too. Keep them company. Put bows on them so they look cute."

Unaccountably, she found herself tearing up at the generousness of his offer, as well as the willingness of others to go along with it. Maybe she'd begun to indulge in a little too much self-pity. Despite everything, there was a significant blessing here to be appreciated. She had the support of her work communities here at the fire station and at the library. People employed by the county emergency services were willing to adjust where they based their services to help her while still keeping the people of Cedar Lodge covered. That was something to be thankful for.

"Do you want to get lunch?" Cole asked with a glance at Emma. "I could use something substantial to eat and I think you could, too."

She nodded. "Good idea. I am hungry." It looked like the task of locating her brother and ensuring his cooperation would be more of a marathon than the quick sprint she'd initially hoped for. Adequate meals were definitely in order to keep up her energy. She knew the police were hard at work following up on all the investigative angles related to the attacks on her. At this particular moment, she wasn't sure what *she* should be doing. But it was apparent she needed to be ready for anything.

Emma looked at the food basket in front of her holding an empty paper sandwich wrapper alongside an empty paper cup that had previously held German potato salad. Cole's suggestion that they visit her favorite deli was much appreciated. The world and her situation in it was no safer, but at least she felt a little bit stronger.

Dill Pickle Deli sat in a quiet location three blocks over from Glacier Street and the downtown area of Cedar Lodge. There was minimal foot traffic through the area, so the chance of the bad guys happening by and seeing Emma didn't seem too great. She and Cole were seated at the very back away from the windows. Nevertheless,

Cole consistently watched the windows and the front door. Somehow he managed to remain vigilant while helping Emma feel relatively safe and relaxed.

"Is there anything you need to grab from your apartment before we head out of town and back to the ranch?" Cole asked.

Emma shook her head. She didn't need a particularly varied wardrobe while she was tromping around the Webb property and she could do laundry while she was there.

They left the table and Cole took their trash to a receptacle in the corner. Emma walked over to look at the desserts in a display case by the cash register, figuring the least she could do to show the Webb family her appreciation for their generous hospitality was to bring back a luscious-looking Black Forest cake.

She was waiting for Cole to come over and let her know if he thought his grandpa would prefer an apple strudel when she decided to check her phone for any notifications she might have missed over the buzz of conversation in the busy deli.

She had no missed calls or texts from Austin. The drop of disappointment gave her a hollowed-out feeling despite her recent meal. Compelled by the need to do something, she tapped the icon for the social media account where her brother had been posting. Both of the posts he'd intended to use as bait to draw out the kidnappers had some clicks of approval from Austin's friends who clearly had no idea what was really going on, along with a few vague comments such as "Enjoy the sunshine," and "Wish I had a long enough break from work to go to the park." But then Emma saw a new comment and she stared at it until Cole came up alongside her.

"Listen to what somebody commented to Austin," she

said. "'Bro, while you were goofing off again I got your tire fixed. Heard you were looking to hire somebody to take care of it. Called and texted but no response and I need to get paid. Need gas money, you know? Waiting here at the Super Mart where you told me to drop it off for a little bit if you want your key back right now. Otherwise, can get it to you later.'"

Attached to the comment was a photo of Austin's car, which Emma had last seen parked outside his friends' apartment with a flat tire, now in the market parking lot with the front driver's side tire repaired.

"Looks like this was posted about fifteen minutes ago," Emma said. "The commenter's name is Lucas Rowe."

"That name sound familiar?" Cole asked.

"No. But I'm out of the loop when it comes to knowing most of Austin's friends." Lucas Rowe's account photo showed a young man about Austin's age. Emma clicked for basic biographical information on the guy. "His security settings are keeping me from seeing very much," she said. "But the account is four years old. It looks legit to me."

Cole gave her a thoughtful look. "Do you want to stay here while I go check things out and see if the car's still there? Or if Austin shows up? Maybe I can talk to Lucas and find out if he has any idea where Austin has been for the last couple of days."

Emma shook her head. "I don't want to stay here without you. I wouldn't feel safe. And if Austin's at the market and he sees me, he won't run away. He'll at least talk to me. I'm sure of it. But he doesn't know you. He's never met you. So if you approach him, there's no telling how he'll respond. I doubt he'd hang around to talk to a stranger, given the circumstances."

"Yeah, but the kidnappers might have seen this post. They could be waiting there."

"I know. And in spite of what Chief Ellis said, I'm sure Officer Donegal is at least monitoring the situation. Maybe the department will send somebody and maybe they won't." She shook her head. "I can't just wait and hope something good happens. I don't want to be foolish and walk into a potential trap of some sort, either. Maybe we could just watch the car from a distance and see if Austin shows up."

"Okay," Cole said. "Let's go."

They stepped outside and took a good look around to make certain it was safe before walking to his truck. It was a short drive to Super Mart, which was in a mixed commercial and residential section of town. It had been a small local grocery store back in the day but was now more of a snack shop with a few common household items and a well-known hot food service counter in the back where you could get everything from take-out plates of meat loaf and potatoes to deep-dish pizza.

Since it was still around lunchtime, the store was doing a brisk business and the narrow parking lot was full when Cole drove by. "I don't want to park in the lot," Cole said. "If the thugs are waiting for us to show up, we'd be easy to spot. Plus, if things go sideways and we need to get away in a hurry, there's a greater possibility we could get blocked in by other vehicles."

"I see Austin's car!" Emma called out, her heart nearly leaping out of her chest when she spotted the vehicle. She twisted in her seat trying to get a better look and hoping to spot her brother as they continued on in the flow of traffic, but ultimately she didn't.

Cole drove around the block and came back. There

weren't any openings where they could park across the street from the store. Half a block farther down the road, on the same side of the street as the store, there was a moderate-size condominium development. The store faced its own parking lot, rather than the street. That meant coming from the direction of the condos they'd be approaching the store from the backside, which seemed safer to Emma.

Cole pulled into the condo parking lot. "If we keep a low profile and approach on foot from this direction, we should be able to get close enough to Austin's car to see what's going on without being noticed." Cole grabbed a weathered hoodie from the back seat of the truck's cab and handed it to Emma. "Let's disguise you a little. Put this on. Pull the hood down to hide your face as much as you can while still being able to see enough to walk."

She slipped on the hoodie, zipped it up and pulled the top down over part of her face. The thing was so oversized on her that it felt like a dress. Cole checked the pistol he'd taken to carrying and then tucked it beneath his waistband at the small of his back beneath his shirt.

Outside of the truck, Emma took a fortifying deep breath. She'd faced danger several times over the last few days, but she had in no way gotten used to it. Nerves tingled uncomfortably across the surface of her skin and her stomach twisted with anxiety and fear. She was scared for herself, scared for her brother and scared for Cole. Had it been wrong of her to allow Cole to put himself in danger on her behalf? She mentally shoved aside the question. It was too late to change anything now.

They walked from the asphalt to the sidewalk and then headed toward the store.

Emma nervously glanced at a couple of people on the sidewalk heading in her direction, both of them carrying

Super Mart take-out packages, but they passed by uneventfully. Then the sudden growl of a car engine caught her attention and her body tensed as she got ready to run for cover. But when she looked over at the street, the driver of the car looked unfamiliar and he didn't seem to be paying any attention to her as he tried to maneuver his vehicle into a parking spot that had just opened up alongside the curb.

She took a deep breath, moved her shoulders a little to loosen them and tried to calm down. If Austin were here she would find him, they would leave together with Cole, and at least one worrisome aspect of her life would finally be over.

She turned her attention to the sidewalk in front of her again. The only person approaching her was a young woman with long dark hair pushing a stroller with one hand and holding an ice cream cone with the other. Hardly a threat.

There was a parklike stretch of grass and shrubs and a few trees at the end of the condominium property where it abutted the Super Mart property. As the woman drew near, Emma stepped off the sidewalk onto the grass to let her and her child pass by. In an instant the woman flung aside the stroller and her ice cream and grabbed Emma by the arms, dragging her backward. The man Emma had noticed parking at the curb a few moments ago was out of his car in a flash and launching himself at Cole before Cole could draw his weapon.

Forced to take multiple steps backward, Emma got tangled in the stroller lying on its side, which she could now see held only empty blankets, and she fell. By the time she righted herself the woman had let go of one of Emma's arms and drawn a gun, pressing it now at the back of Emma's neck. "Stand right here," the woman ground out her words. "If you fight with me I'll kill you."

A car barreled down the street toward them before braking with a loud squeal. For a few seconds Emma hoped it might bring help, but her heart sank when she saw Ponytail Guy sitting behind the wheel and Bald Guy in the passenger seat. They must be working with the criminals who'd just taken Cole and Emma by surprise.

Heart thundering in her chest, Emma shifted her gaze to Cole. He was fiercely punching the creep who'd jumped him, although the assailant appeared to be giving as good as he got in return. Trembling with fear, Emma knew that once Ponytail Guy and Bald Guy jumped out of their car and joined the fight, it would be all over for Emma and Cole. She would be taken hostage and for all she knew Cole might be killed. No way would she let that happen.

Angry determination fueled a shot of energy that surged through her body. She twisted and jabbed her fist at the woman holding on to her, obviously taking the attacker by surprise as she didn't throw up any kind of defensive move before Emma's punch connected with her jaw. Moving on instinct, barely thinking before taking desperate action, Emma grabbed a fistful of the woman's hair and yanked it downward while at the same time grabbing the attacker's gun and twisting her hand and wrist in a desperate attempt to force the woman to drop the weapon.

In return for her efforts, Emma got kicked hard at the side of her knee, causing her to lose her balance and fall again, but this time the attacker fell with her. Looking beside her she saw the woman's gun on the ground, but before Emma could crawl to it the assailant pinned her face-down so she couldn't move. Emma heard gunshots fired in the direction she'd last seen Cole. Terrified that he'd been struck, she turned to look in his direction. At the same time she felt the attacker who was holding her down shift her weight as if she were reaching for her gun in the grass. Emma quickly took advantage of the situation to shove the woman off her, roll aside and then scramble to her feet. Her head was swimming. In the blur of movement and color, she recognized Cole with his gun drawn. She also saw people coming from the direction of the store. She heard a sound that might have been a siren but she wasn't sure.

Unsteady on her feet, she hesitated in the moment of confusion and disorientation and felt two hands grasp her ankles and yank hard until she fell forward and was on the ground again. In the next instant she was being dragged across the grass, toward the street and the car waiting with the thugs to grab her and drive her away. Emma screamed and kicked and tried to twist around so she no longer had her face in the grass. The dragging stopped and something hard, like maybe a gun, struck her on the side of the head. Stunned, she fought to stay conscious.

She heard gunshots again, this time coming from Cole's direction instead of toward it. The woman who'd been dragging her seemed to give up on the job. The sound she'd heard in the distance was definitely sirens and they were growing louder. She heard running foot-steps on the sidewalk and slamming car doors and then the roar of a single car engine as it sounded like the two attackers had gotten into the vehicle with Ponytail Guy and Bald Guy before it sped away.

"Hey," Cole said softly. He was now kneeling in the grass by her head.

"Don't worry, I'm all right," Emma said, though her voice was shaky and weak and she didn't think she sounded at all convincing. She began shoving herself to a sitting position.

"Don't move," Cole cautioned.

"We're not at work, so you're not my boss."

She heard him laugh quietly. When she turned to get a look at him, she was relieved to see that he appeared to be okay. "You didn't get shot."

"No," he said. "The baldheaded attacker aimed at me, but he missed."

"Hey, are you two all right?" A stranger came up to them, but after taking a moment to focus her eyes, Emma could see that he was wearing a policeman's badge on a thick lanyard, even though he wasn't dressed in a uniform. Probably an undercover cop. She didn't recognize him.

"I'm okay," Emma said, getting to her feet. "I'll just have a headache for a while."

Two cop cars pulled up to the curb and silenced their sirens. Kris Volker and another officer hurried over to them. The undercover cop gave the patrol officers the specifics on the vehicle the four attackers had escaped in, as well as descriptions of the assailants. The other vehicle used by the assailants had been left behind. Volker relayed the information over his radio and then he and the other patrol officer left to try to chase down the criminals' car.

"Officer Donegal saw the comment on your brother's post and she thought it seemed suspicious," the undercover cop said to Emma. "There wasn't time to prep anything elaborate or put together any kind of surveillance team, but Chief Ellis had me come over to Super Mart and watch for a little while in case something significant happened."

Emma smiled faintly. It looked as if the police chief had

changed his mind about reacting to Austin's posts. Or at least about reacting to the comment on the most recent one.

"Apparently somebody saw your altercation out here and called it in. I didn't actually see it. I was watching the front of the store and keeping an eye on your brother's car to see who might be inside it or who might approach it."

"Did you see anybody?" Emma asked.

The cop shook his head. "No. The chief is sympathetic to what's going on with your brother. But the only reason he had me respond to this comment today was because I happened to be in the station and available." The cop gestured toward the street where the latest criminal's car remained. "So, looks like there are at least four thugs determined to come after you now."

"It does." Emma nodded her aching head in agreement.

This had obviously been a setup. Whether the commenter Lucas Rowe was legitimate and the thugs had just happened to see his comment, or if the comment itself was fabricated by Royce Walker's criminal gang, she didn't know. Perhaps it had been a ruse with the intention of drawing out Austin, herself, or possibly the both of them.

Just when she thought things couldn't get worse, they did. Every time. She wanted out of the nightmare her life had become. She was furious with her brother for making things so much worse despite his good intentions. Even so, there was no way she'd leave Cedar Lodge to escape the danger without him. She glanced at Cole, who was talking with the undercover officer. When she did find Austin, and the time came for them to leave town for a safe location, it would break her heart when she had to say goodbye to Cole.

ELEVEN

"I have to do *something*," Emma insisted. "And going back to the apartment to talk to Austin's friends again is the only thing I can think of."

"Don't you want to go back to the ranch and lay low for a while?" Cole didn't want to sound pushy, but that was precisely what he wanted her to do in the aftermath of the attack outside Super Mart. Ultimately, however, what she would do next was her decision to make.

"I want to go back to the ranch and rest, believe me. But not just yet."

The two of them were sitting in Cole's truck still parked at the condominium parking lot. The undercover cop had taken their statements so at least they didn't have to worry about going back to the police station to follow up on that. It was beyond unnerving to know that there were now at least four thugs trying to grab Emma. The fact that they hadn't been able to gain complete control over her and spirit her away was due in large part to Emma's determination to fight back with all that she had when they came after her.

The criminals' getaway car had been found abandoned roughly twenty-five minutes after the attack. Of course it had been reported stolen, but maybe there would be fingerprints inside that could be used to identify the attackers and perhaps that could somehow help the cops locate them. Cole was willing to lean into hope because right now that was about all they had.

"Austin's car had been parked right outside the apartment building," Emma said, interrupting his thoughts. "Benny and Shawn must have seen something. Maybe they saw Austin and talked to him. Maybe they saw Lucas and talked to him when he showed up to repair the tire. Assuming he's a real person."

They still had no clear answer regarding Lucas and whether he was actually a friend of Austin's or he was just a false online identity the Walker gang used when they needed one.

"All right, let's go talk to Benny and Shawn again." Cole started up the engine and drove onto the street. They arrived at the apartment building a few minutes later.

"Maybe I should wait at the back door in case Austin's in there and he tries to run away," Emma said as they parked.

"I think not." Cole took a look around. "It would be better if we stayed together."

"Okay, you're probably right."

He glanced over and Emma was rubbing the area around her collarbone. "If you keep getting jumped, that bone bruise is never going to heal."

"It's more annoying than painful." She gave him a half smile. "It will be one more thing to yell at my brother about when I finally catch up with him. Would be nice if that happened within the next few minutes."

"Hopefully at least one of the guys will be home. I wouldn't count on Austin being here."

"I don't see any security cameras," Emma said as they

approached the apartments. She glanced at the building and then over at the spot in the parking lot where Austin's car had previously been parked.

"Excuse me." Cole stepped in front of Emma as they approached the door and then he knocked on it. If someone came out swinging, or shooting, he wanted to be a layer of protection between the assailant and Emma.

Feeling edgy and impatient after getting assaulted outside the Super Mart, he waited just a few seconds before knocking on the door again, a little more forcefully this time.

"I'm coming," a voice called out and then the door was yanked open. Benny stood there with headphones on, but he'd slid the earpiece away from one of his ears so he could hear better. "You guys are back," he said in a friendly tone. "What's up?"

"Is my brother here?" Emma demanded, pushing past Cole and inviting herself into the apartment without waiting for an answer.

There wasn't much Cole could do other than follow her in and stay close by her side.

Emma barreled through the small living room to a narrow door beside the kitchen that led to a tiny unfenced back patio. She shoved the door open and stepped outside, looking around. By now Cole was right beside her. A narrow strip of grass stretched across the ground behind the apartments. Cole and Emma looked in both directions.

"I don't see anyone," Cole said, assuming they were looking for Emma's brother. He looked down. "Doesn't appear that the grass has recently been stomped on."

Emma nodded that she'd heard him, and then hurried down the stretch of lawn toward the street for a look anyway. Cole went with her. He understood the compulsion to see things for yourself when you were worried. After they stood for a moment and she looked up and down the street a couple of times, she turned to him. "Guess you're right. He wasn't here."

Cole nodded. "Let's go back and talk to Benny."

They returned to the apartment's back door where Benny stood waiting, his headphones removed, a quizzical expression on his face. "Why would you think I'd hide Austin?" he asked as Cole and Emma stepped back inside and Benny closed and then locked the door behind them. "After you came by last time, I started keeping a closer eye on the local news. I know you've been attacked. I *really* get it that Austin must be in serious danger."

"Have you gotten any ideas of where he might be staying?" Cole asked.

Benny shook his head. "No. I've talked with a few friends and nobody's seen him."

"Where's Shawn?" Emma asked, looking around.

"Working. Help desk at Montana Computer Source."

"Have you been here all day?"

Benny nodded. "I work from home. Medical billing. Not always exciting, but the pay is good and I don't have to deal with irate customers like Shawn does."

"Did you see who came and got Austin's car?"

"Somebody got his car?" Benny raised his eyebrows. "That's news to me."

"So you didn't see anybody?" Cole jumped in. "Nobody knocked on the door, maybe asked for a key to the car?"

Benny frowned and shook his head.

"Do you know someone named Lucas Rowe?" Emma asked. "He posted something on Austin's social media account today about coming by to repair Austin's flat tire for him. Do you know anything about that?"

"I don't have any friends named Lucas. I don't know if Austin does."

"Being tech guys I'm surprised you two don't have security cameras," Cole said, not certain if he trusted the guy. Maybe he was just good at acting friendly and helpful.

Benny pointed at a couple of small cameras on shelves in the living room. "We turn these on when nobody's home. We might buy outside ones eventually, but there haven't been any break-ins around here since we moved in. Both of us are trying to save money for some better furniture and maybe a trip to Hawaii." He shrugged. "Neighbors might have cameras."

Emma sighed heavily. "Thanks, Benny."

"Look, if you want to check in the closets and under the bed to see if Austin's here you can. He's not, but if it'll make you feel better, be my guest."

Emma shook her head. "That's all right. I believe you."

"Well, I'm worried about him, too, you know. I've called and texted him a few more times but got nothing in response. I'm sure you saw the social media stuff he supposedly posted. I didn't respond to it because it seemed weird and out of character for him. I kind of thought his account had been hacked."

Emma didn't explain the situation with Austin's social media so Cole didn't talk any further about it, either.

After they left the apartment, Cole turned to Emma. "Do you want to knock on the neighbors' doors and see if they have some security video?"

She shook her head. "I think I'll send a text to Kris Volker and see if he wants to come by and talk to the neighbors. I doubt they'd want to cooperate with us very much. I'd be suspicious if some stranger showed up at my door asking for video footage, so I wouldn't blame them. But maybe they'd talk to the police. Right now I'm starting to feel pretty tired and I'd like to go back to the ranch. Seems like everything's catching up with me."

"Sorry you didn't get to yell at your brother in person," Cole teased her as they got into the truck.

She smiled weakly in return. "I can call him and yell at him over the phone even if I'm just leaving a recording. That will probably be therapeutic enough."

"Okay."

"I'd like to go by my apartment to get my SUV and take it out to the ranch since it looks like I'll be staying there for a little longer."

"All right."

Cole couldn't help noticing how sad and exhausted she looked. It was a miserable feeling not being able to make things better for her. And it was a frightening and unsettling feeling knowing another attempt at kidnapping Emma was inevitable, and the attackers—all *four* of them now—were still at large.

"Let me make dinner tomorrow night," Emma said after the evening meal at the ranch. *Assuming I'm here and not out pursuing a lead on finding my brother.*

Lauren and Brent, who had made tonight's dinner, both uttered mild exclamations of protest. "You don't have to do that," Brent said. "Lauren and I both enjoy cooking."

"And I enjoy eating." Grandpa laughed at his own joke and slapped his hand down on the kitchen table. "Those stuffed bell peppers were delicious."

They were all in the cozy dining room beside the kitchen, seated at the sturdy, aged oak table. There were family photos plus decorative objects on the walls, along with oil lamps and candles on the shelves that gave Emma the impression the power probably went out fairly often in rough weather. Even with a backup generator, smaller sources of light could come in handy while going through the steps to get the generator going.

There were also plenty of books jammed onto shelves in the dining room, as well as most other rooms in the house. The Webb family like to read. Emma had already been approached about offering suggestions on good books, and she'd been happy to help.

"I'll probably be around all or most of the day tomorrow," Emma pressed on with her topic. "Planning a nice dinner will give me something to do. It will also offer me at least one small way to repay your kindness."

The family again started up with their polite protests.

"Please don't tell me you're going to make stationhouse chili," Cole said in a joking tone of complaint. "I've had enough of that to hold me for a while."

Emma indulged in an affronted lift of her chin. "I'll make something fascinating and you'll love it."

"You've seen the storehouse of food we keep around here," Grandpa said. "Feel free to make use of any of it."

Emma grinned at him. "Thank you."

On their arrival back at the ranch, Cole had brought up the idea of Emma taking a day off to rest and recover from all she'd been through while he worked an eight-hour shift. She'd rebuffed the idea at first, saying that it made her feel as if she were giving up on finding Austin. But in the end, she admitted she didn't actually have any specific new plan for how to find him and staying at the ranch to rest and recover might be a good idea after all.

Everyone started to get up from the table, and Emma quickly set about helping to clear the plates.

"I can take care of this," Cole told her when they ended up together in the kitchen. "It's my turn to do them. I just need to hand-wash a couple of pans and put the rest in the dishwasher."

"All right," Emma said, grabbing a dish towel. "You wash the pans and I'll dry."

When they'd returned from town, Cole had gone out to help his grandpa repair a gate. Brent and Lauren had spent a couple of hours filling online orders and packaging their beautifully dyed wool yarn to ship out the next morning. Emma knew there was more work to get done after dinner while there was still daylight, most of it having to do with tending the livestock. The Webb family worked hard all day, and while Emma hadn't quite known how to help earlier, she figured tomorrow she could feed and water the animals if someone told her exactly what to do.

Cole scraped the plates clean and set them in the washer, then rolled up his sleeves and filled the sink with hot, soapy water. It felt good for Emma to have something physical and practical to do to help take her mind off her brother. And her parents. The last she'd heard from them, the authorities had told her mom and dad they believed they were close to finding Royce Walker. Maybe it was fact and maybe it was wishful thinking. They were still being afforded round-the-clock protection, so the possibility that Walker or one of his thugs would come after her dad seemed remote, but it was not completely out of the realm of possibility.

Cole washed a pan and handed it to Emma to dry. It was warm to the touch, as were Cole's fingertips as they brushed against hers. Her heart began to beat faster. Cole looked at her, she caught his gaze, and he didn't turn away for several lingering moments that had Emma holding her breath.

The paramedic had been impressive from the very first time she'd seen him working. She'd been a volunteer EMT back then, and she'd been added to his ambulance to assist on the response to a collision out on the state highway involving a semi and multiple passenger vehicles.

It had been bad. She'd seen Cole in action, watched him saving lives and making critical decisions under incredible pressure. Intense and focused, but also calm and relatively cool at the same time. She'd admired him then, and later when she'd gone from volunteer to part-time paid fire department employee, she'd enjoyed working with him. But he'd always been professional to the point of being aloof at times, which was fine. He was eight years older than her. Was a combat veteran. It wasn't like they'd had anything in common beyond working together. She hadn't been romantically attracted to him. But now, things had changed.

Working beside him and doing something as mundane as washing dishes had her thinking about how she'd gotten used to being around him, not as distracted coworkers, but as two people who were connected on a deeper level. People who really were connecting with each other and becoming a team, though the word *team* seemed too tepid and emotionless.

For the longest time Emma had been afraid to develop a true, deep romantic relationship. Her identity had been fake. She'd been living a lie in a way, and how could she keep that from someone she truly cared about? When and if they learned the truth, how could they not feel betrayed and wonder what else she'd kept hidden from them?

But now, well, there was no denying that it was horrible

how her family had been thrown into danger and disarray with their new identities and location being uncovered. But it also meant she wouldn't have that burden of holding back a big secret from Cole. Maybe she could dare to want a personal relationship with him. And there was so much about his recent behavior that made her think he felt that way about her.

"It's strange to realize that I've known you for years, worked countless shifts with you, but I didn't really know you until now," Emma ventured. It wasn't like they'd had much opportunity to talk about themselves on a personal level over the last few days. They'd been busy keeping themselves alive while trying to track down her brother. And it was clear that Cole was in danger now, too. The bad guys had to see him as a threat. Never mind an obstacle to them easily grabbing Emma and dragging her off to a situation she didn't want to think about.

Cole glanced at her over his shoulder, his hands still in the soapy water washing another pan. "My work life is separate from my personal life. I like to keep it that way."

"Well, that has certainly changed," Emma countered, making sure to add a lighthearted, teasing tone to her comment. While at the same time realizing that she didn't feel at all lighthearted about the topic at hand. That topic being the possibility of the two of them continuing on as friends after this horrible situation with Royce Walker's thug employees was resolved. Hopefully with Walker recovered by the US Marshals service and the criminal and his gang members all locked up in prison where they belonged.

"You're in danger," Cole said, still not looking directly at her. "I'm going to do everything I can to make sure nothing happens to you. I'd do that for anybody."

The hope that had started to well up in her heart began to deflate a little. But then she thought of the moments they'd shared. The gazes that had lasted longer than they would have if either of them were not particularly important to the other. The embraces that had likewise lingered to the extent that Emma had been sure they'd meant something. They'd absolutely meant something to her.

The feeling of closeness right now as they washed dishes together was something new and different. Something that seemed to be strengthening a connection between her and Cole. She'd stood with Cole washing dishes countless times in the breakroom at the fire station when crew members working a shift through dinner had come together to make and share a meal. They'd talked and joked and she was certain her fingers must have brushed his at some point and it had meant nothing.

But now there was *something* between them. She was sure of it.

For a moment she considered dropping the subject for now. Maybe pressing Cole for an acknowledgment that he felt something too would ruin things.

No.

Emma Burke, who'd been forced to take on the surname of Hayes to protect herself and her family, was tired of hiding and holding back. She'd done that since she was fifteen and was relocated in Cedar Lodge. She had friends to hang around with growing up but she hadn't really had the *close* friendships she'd craved because she had such a big secret in her life. That secret had been a roadblock to romantic relationships because she just couldn't see herself building a long-term relationship on a lie. She hadn't been able to stop herself from worrying about what would happen if she were to keep the lie and marry someone and later they learned the truth. What would happen to the trust that had existed between them? Would it be forever broken?

Enough with hiding. Enough with worrying about what someone would think. Despite all the horribleness going on with these terrifying attacks, at least she was free to be herself now. Free to speak without having to second-guess everything.

"Why are you so afraid to get close to anybody?" Emma boldly asked. Admittedly, and rather selfishly, she wanted to know why he didn't want to admit that he'd gotten emotionally close to *her*. Because she was sure that he had. But now she found herself thinking about how he was at the fire station. He'd been friendly enough with her, at times. But then other times he would seem to withdraw. She'd just figured it was a personality quirk. Hadn't thought all that much about it. Until now.

"You already know the reason why I've stayed out of serious relationships," she said. "Having a secret identity will do that. What's your reason?"

Cole stilled, leaving his hands in the soapy water. He looked out the window over the sink and didn't say anything for a while.

Emma's heart sank. She'd obviously struck a nerve. She'd hurt this man who'd only tried to help her. She'd been so caught up in herself and what she wanted that she hadn't bothered to consider that an obviously strong man would still have feelings. And a right to privacy.

"I'm sorry," she said, her emotions now a whir of pain and regret. She'd pushed too hard. At this point she wasn't certain which was more painful, realizing that she'd misread the situation and he wasn't interested in her romantically, or knowing that she'd hurt and possibly embarrassed a very kind man. A person had the right to keep their own confidence. She should know that better than anybody.

"I'm talking too much," she added lamely.

"What else is new?" Cole responded.

Emma let out a breath, relieved to hear the familiar teasing tone in his voice, though it sounded a bit forced.

He handed her the last pan and then dried his hands. "We work together, Emma. When we're on the ambulance, I'm your supervisor. That's a problem when things get too personal. I don't have a great romantic track record, and I don't know that I have it in me to try again. I like my life the way it is and I'm not looking for anybody. I'm sorry."

Emma wanted to argue every point, but she bit her tongue. Apparently she had misinterpreted his actions. She'd read too much into them. She'd only *thought* those moments were meaningful. They hadn't actually been. Well, they'd only been meaningful for *her*.

Cole walked to the door leading outside from the kitchen, grabbed a cowboy hat off a hook on the wall, and then put the hat on his head. "I'm going to go help Lauren and Brent and Grandpa get the animals settled down for the night. Why don't you kick back in the living room and rest for a while."

His tone was different now. Distant, and somewhat like he sounded when they were at work. Which made the whole situation more painful because it proved to her that they had reached a point where they were closer and more open with each other and now that was gone.

Hugging her stomach, Emma headed toward the living room. Already, she felt a severing of the connection between them. How would it feel to be around him now that things had changed? And how was she supposed to let go of the hope that they'd continue to spend as much time together as possible after she found Austin, and the thugs were captured?

She blinked back tears and wiped at her eyes, determined to clear away every trace of her sadness before anyone returned to the house. She was getting ahead of herself worrying about her future with Cole, anyway. She might not even have a future, period. She and Austin were still in danger. Another attack could come at any time. It was foolish of her to assume that none of the attacks against her could be successful. Or fatal if she got caught in the crossfire. Turning her attention away from danger and toward imagining a future with Cole wasn't something she could afford to do, anyway. It was time to pull herself back together and carry on.

TWELVE

Cole sat at a desk at the fire station the next day and tapped the send button for the medical supply reorder he'd just completed. It was early afternoon and after a busy morning things had slowed down enough that he had time to take care of some administrative work.

As soon as his restock was digitally on its way, however, his thoughts turned back to Emma. He'd been thinking about her since he left the ranch early this morning. In fact, he'd been thinking about her pretty much all the time since he'd stumbled upon her abandoned car beside the lake three days ago.

Their conversation in the kitchen yesterday evening had been unsettling and it still weighed on his mind.

Up to that point he'd managed to convince himself that he wasn't *really* romantically interested in her and that she wasn't seriously interested in him. The two of them were simply caught up in a highly emotional situation with her life in danger and him doing his best to protect her, and that kind of situation was bound to stir up emotions. But those emotions would be fleeting.

Maybe that was true. But then again, maybe it wasn't. Maybe the feelings of attraction and connection she'd awakened in him had more substance than he'd wanted to admit.

It had been hard to fall asleep last night as he'd found himself questioning what he personally wanted out of life for the first time in ages. At some point he must have stopped imagining a future with a wife and children. Emma had proven to be the strong kind of woman a man could rely on. There was no escaping that she was attractive. She had a faith life that was similar to his own.

So what was holding him back? The work situation, with him being her supervisor, was a significant problem. But what else? He didn't want to make the same mistake his mother had and marry someone who faked a depth of character and trustworthiness they didn't truly possess. But did he really want to use that as an excuse to never take the chance of falling in love again? Was that really something he wanted, or was he just continuing with it because it had become habit and it was easier to keep his distance?

He glanced at his phone on the desk, thinking about calling her just to make sure everything was all right. But she or Grandpa would call if there was a problem, and he needed to get his focus back on work. It would probably be better to wait until he could talk to her in person after the end of his shift, though he had no idea what he would say. He figured he'd know when he saw her. Maybe by then he'd be clearer on what he wanted.

He'd been updating the departmental calendar with the next round of free basic first aid courses to be offered to the community when his phone rang. It was Emma.

He tapped the screen. "Everything okay?"

"Better than okay!" she replied happily. "I heard from Austin! He finally called me. And that's why I'm calling you. I'd like to invite him here to your ranch if that's okay. I know technically it's your grandfather's place, but I wanted to talk to you about it first."

Cole felt a stirring of unease in the back of his mind. "Why is Austin reaching out to you now when he didn't do it before? What's prompting this?"

"He just found out about the assault outside Super Mart and that I was in the middle of it all. He says he's done with those stupid social media posts. He doesn't know anybody named Lucas Rowe and he didn't make any arrangement to get his tire repaired. So it turns out that actually was a setup to draw *me* out so they could try to grab me. The police impounded his car while they check for fingerprints or any other useful evidence that might have been left behind."

So the criminals who'd been hunting Emma were not just relentless, they were clever and technically sophisticated, too. That didn't bode well.

"How is it that Austin just now found out about the Super Mart attack?" Cole asked. "I thought he was following his own social media posts and he was on top of things."

"He's been staying with a friend in their family's fishing cabin and that friend drove him into town to take the photos and make the social media posts. Phone reception where he's been staying is almost nonexistent."

That was believable. Lack of phone connectivity around Cedar Lodge was a topic almost as common as the constantly changing weather.

"Why does he need to come to the ranch? Why can't he remain at the cabin where he's been staying?"

"Because I want to see him," Emma said, sounding confused or maybe even offended by his question. "And I want us to spend time together while we figure out what to do next. Where we should go."

She might leave. Cole's stomach knotted.

"You're safe at the ranch," he said. "I don't want to take any chances on having that change."

"What do you mean?" she demanded. "Do you not trust him? Do you think Sergeant Newman was right from the start? Do you really believe Austin sold out my family and he'll sell me out to the kidnappers as well?"

Cole wasn't sure what he thought. He only knew he didn't want to take any risks with Emma's safety. "What if the thugs have gotten to Austin and they're using him to get to you?" Cole asked. "What if they had a gun pointed at him while he made the call to you just now? I think we need to slow down with this. Take smaller steps."

There was silence on the other end of the phone. "Talk to me, Emma," Cole finally said.

"I'm thinking." She sounded tense, but no longer angry. "I want to see him as soon as I can, but you're right and we need to be cautious. Maybe I could meet up with him someplace in town. Like a coffee shop. If I got there first, I could see if he showed up alone or not. If things seem okay, we can head out to the ranch from there. Or he and I could find someplace else to stay. I will not leave him on his own."

"I still think that sounds dangerous." Cole rubbed his forehead while he thought for a moment. "How about I meet Austin here at the fire station. It's a public place with other people around, which is a good start. I can talk to him and if everything seems okay, I'll drive him to the ranch. I can watch for anyone tailing us along the way."

"Works for me. I'll call him to set it up."

"And I'll call Grandpa to make sure he's okay with your brother staying at the ranch. I'm pretty sure he will be."

"Thank you," Emma said.

"Right," Cole said, not wanting to accept her gratitude because he wasn't certain that bringing Austin to the ranch was a good idea. But in the end, what Emma did was completely her choice. At least if there was trouble at the ranch, Cole would be fighting to protect Emma in familiar territory. He just hoped this reconciliation with Austin was not a dangerous setup that would lead the criminal gang members directly to Emma.

"I'm so happy to see you and know that you're okay!" Emma hugged her brother while continuing to ignore his tearful apologies.

"I'm so sorry, Emma," Austin sobbed into her shoulder. "I thought putting up the posts was a good idea, but it was stupid. I never meant for you to get hurt."

"I'm all right. I got tackled in that little park behind Super Mart, something I *never* imagined would happen to me, but I'm okay," she said in a teasing tone, hoping to lighten her brother's misery and regret.

In the midst of his crying, she heard a little bit of a laugh and it eased the ache in her own heart. She'd been so frustrated with Austin, but she hadn't blamed him. Not for anything. At the end of the day, the fault for all of the terrible things that had been happening lay with the murderous criminal Royce Walker. He committed the horrible crime that set all of these recent attacks in motion.

Austin released her and stepped back. Emma took another good look at him. They were in the living room at the Webb family ranch where he and Cole had just arrived. Of course her brother didn't look hugely different from the last time she'd seen him a couple of weeks ago, but even in the soft light of the ranch house she noticed the worry and exhaustion in his face. And she noticed when hugging him that he felt thinner, like he'd lost weight.

"Welcome to our home." Cole's grandfather stepped up to introduce himself and shake hands with Austin before moving on to introduce Lauren and Brent.

Austin offered up a nervous, self-conscious smile. "Hi."

"So, who exactly is this friend you've been staying with for the last three days?" Emma asked, leading the way to a sofa and gesturing at Austin to sit down beside her.

"You remember my friend Dave?" he asked hopefully.

Sadly, she did not. Maybe Dave had been at her parents' house with Austin at some point and they'd been introduced and she hadn't really paid much attention. "I'm afraid I don't."

His hopeful expression dimmed.

Emma had paid attention to her own interests and ignored his, using the five-year age difference between herself and Austin to rationalize her detachment. *Dear Lord, please forgive me.* She was determined to change her attitude and never let herself behave that way again.

"You were staying with Dave?" she prompted.

"Yeah. His family has a cabin up on Sawtooth Ridge. He told his parents he wanted to go up and do some hiking and fishing and they were cool with that and let him have the key. He didn't tell them about me, though."

Emma nodded. "Tell me, were you at Mom and Dad's house when I was there? The day they had to leave? I saw somebody in the backyard and later I thought it might have been you."

Austin raised his eyebrows. "It might have been me. Man, if you were there, I wish I'd known." He shook his head. "I'd been crashing with Benny and Shawn for a couple of days and got tired of it. My car had a flat tire so I walked to the house. When I got there, I could see the front door had been kicked open." His voice had become shaky with emotion and he cleared his throat. "I called out for Mom and Dad. Nobody answered and I went inside. The house was empty and I was sure that Royce Walker's people had finally located them after all these years. I went out in the backyard, just frantic and wanting to believe I was wrong and I'd find them outside pulling weeds or something.

"When I heard somebody in the house I was scared that the Walker gang members had returned for some reason after already grabbing Mom and Dad. I took off running and didn't look back." Austin drew a deep breath and ran his fingers through his hair. "I kept calling Mom and Dad and finally I got through to Mom. While I was calling and neither of them was answering, I kept praying they were all right and thinking about how this was probably my fault. Sorry I took so long to return your calls, but after I got your first message and knew you were okay I was more focused on our parents. And on figuring out what I should do next."

Emma thought back to Newman's accusations that Austin had sold out their parents. The deputy had made it sound as if he and his witness protection task force associates had a fleshed-out theory regarding Austin betraying their parents and that they had some kind of actual evidence. But she'd never seen that evidence. Never heard it described specifically or in detail. In her heart she'd trusted Austin, but seeing and hearing him now, how could anyone doubt his sincerity? She certainly didn't.

"Why do you blame yourself?" she pressed. "Is there

some specific post that haunts you or was it just the random messages or comments you posted?"

Austin twisted his hands in his lap. "When we first moved here when I was ten, I was just so mad. I was supposed to cut myself off from all my friends. I was supposed to get used to being in cowboy country when I was just starting to skateboard." He looked at Cole and his family. "No offense. I've got nothing against cowboys now. But I didn't fit into all of the cowboy lifestyle as a kid."

"No offense taken," Cole said. Like the rest of his family, he was seated in the living room, listening to the conversation while a fragrant pot of coffee finished brewing in the kitchen.

Austin turned back to his sister. "I broke the rules. I contacted my friends down in California. I chatted with them while we played online games and I made snarky comments about where we live. But I never mentioned the actual name of Cedar Lodge. Eventually I outgrew all that, but as I got older it stuck in the back of my mind. When I got a little smarter I felt really bad. It was stupid of me. When I saw our front door kicked in and Mom and Dad were missing, all that old regret and guilt came flooding back. I assumed it was all my fault and that somehow I'd put our lives in danger so it was my responsibility to fix things."

Emma leaned back into the couch and wrapped an arm around his shoulder. Which felt awkward, since he was quite a bit taller than her. "Even after I told you that Mom and Dad had been in contact with our relatives, you still blamed yourself?"

Austin turned to her. "Yes. I know what I did, and it just seems more likely that I'm the one who messed up and said something that I shouldn't have, rather than our grandparents."

"Turns out creating a new identity and cutting yourself off completely from everybody in your past isn't easy for anybody," Emma said. "Not even for adults and not even when you know it could help save your life. Who knows if what you posted caused all this trouble or whether it's happened because one of our grandparents mentioned something to somebody and that's how the Walker people found us? However it happened, I know Mom and Dad don't want you to blame yourself." She squeezed her arm around his shoulder. "We need to call them tonight."

"Okay." He turned to her. "What happens next?"

"So, Royce Walker escaped custody."

Austin's eyes grew round. "Which means we're right back to where we were before. We've got to go back into hiding and get new identities all over again."

"Well, we are going to have to do *something*. We can't just go back to the lives we had four days ago. We'd be sitting ducks. Dad is still the key to putting Royce away for murder. You and I are vulnerable to being kidnapped and used as bargaining chips so Dad doesn't testify." Emma looked at Cole, who'd been listening with apparent interest. "We'll be out of your hair as soon as we can figure out the best place for us to go." She shifted her gaze to the floor because looking at Cole right now hurt too much. He'd told her they didn't have a future together, and she accepted that. But the feelings she had for him hadn't gone away despite her best efforts to dismiss them. She would miss Cole after she left town. She'd miss him terribly.

She looked up and his grandpa had his gaze settled on Cole before finally turning it to Emma. "You and your brother are welcome to stay here at the ranch for as long as you like. In fact, it might be wise to take your time before you make a move."

"Thank you."

"I'm going to get a cup of coffee," Lauren said after no one spoke for a moment. "Anybody else wants some, follow me into the kitchen." She stood up and started heading in that direction.

"This is actually a pretty cool place," Austin said to Emma as he glanced around the interior of the ranch house. He looked out the window at the surrounding pastures and forest. "What kind of animals do they have out here?"

"We have horses and sheep and goats and some chickens," Brent answered. "You want to go have a look around? I could use some help gathering eggs."

Austin grinned. "Sure."

Cole got to his feet. "I'll go out to the stables and get everything settled down for the night." He headed for the door without even a glance at Emma.

Emma was drawn to the scent of fresh coffee, but at the last minute she decided to follow Cole out to the stables. She had no idea what was going to happen next in her life, or how quickly she and Austin would leave the ranch. She wanted to take advantage of what might be her last opportunity for a private conversation with Cole.

Regret that she'd spent so much time around the man without realizing what a good person he was still gnawed at her. She'd spent a good part of last night and pretty much all of today plagued with "what-ifs" as she thought about him. What if she'd taken a closer look at him sooner? What if it hadn't taken threats to her life for her to realize that she really had grown to care for him? The fact that they worked together didn't seem insurmountable. What if they just worked different shifts? Or if one of them took a job with the county fire and rescue department?

None of that mattered now, and her heart ached thinking about the fact that she'd leave soon and never see him again. And as much as it hurt to admit it, he hadn't exactly jumped at the opportunity for a relationship with her when she'd brought it up. In fact, his reaction had been the opposite. And thinking about that reaction last night and today was what brought her to this point of following him up toward the stables.

"Hey, slow down," she called out as he reached the corral fence beside the stables.

Cole stopped and turned, a guarded expression on his face.

"All that time we worked together and you never could slow down so I didn't have to jog to keep up. You and those long legs."

He leaned against the corral railing. "Really? You came out here to fuss at me about how I walk?" He leaned down for a moment to scratch the dogs, who'd ambled out from the stables to greet him.

Emma planted both feet in front of him and brushed her hair out of her eyes. Dark clouds were rolling in and the breeze had gotten brisk, blowing tendrils of hair across her face.

"Actually, I came out here to apologize."

"For what?"

Embarrassed, she cleared her throat. "I'm sorry for what I said to you while we were washing dishes last night. I shouldn't have pushed you. I had no right. I don't know anything about your life's history and it isn't my business anyway." Realizing that she'd started to flail her hands as she spoke, she now crossed her arms over her chest. "Look,

I just really appreciate all you've done for me, and seeing this other side of you, experiencing some of your personality that you keep hidden, well, I just really liked that."

Cole tilted his head slightly and a warm smile spread across his lips. It appeared he was about to say something when he straightened his head and his entire body stiffened. He stared at something behind Emma and then grabbed the collars of both dogs. "Take Liza and Misty and shut them up in the tack room in the stable so they don't get shot. You stay there, too."

Emma took control of the dogs.

Cole reached for the gun tucked in his waistband.

Emma turned. Four figures who'd just emerged from the tree line on the other side of the property were rapidly moving toward the ranch house.

Her stomach dropped. "They've found us."

THIRTEEN

"I'll take care of the dogs, but I'm not going to stay here and hide." Emma turned and hurried toward the stables with the animals.

Certain she meant it, Cole caught up with her and they rushed to get the dogs secured before racing toward the house.

Lord! Protect my family!

Slowing down to call someone in the house made no sense when Cole was this close and he was armed and he'd actually be able to *do* something as soon as he got there. Emma was hot on his heels, so he called out to her, "Phone 9-1-1!"

He veered toward the back of the house. Had the thugs spotted him and Emma by the corral? He didn't think so. If they had, they probably would have started shooting.

The criminals were close to the front door. If Cole went in through the back he could approach them from inside the house and take them by surprise. Racing into the house and yelling for Grandpa and Lauren to grab their guns might be the exact thing to instigate a shootout with the assailants that would get them all killed. He needed a smart strategy if he wanted this to end well.

He reached the back of the house and pressed his ear against the door to listen.

Emma caught up with him, still on the line with the emergency dispatcher.

Cole held his fingers up to his lips to indicate that she should be quiet and then gestured for her to move back. Instead of walking away, she ended her call and mouthed the words "they're on their way."

Even so, their response would take a while. The Webb family ranch was on the backside of the lake in a sparsely populated area with very little crime. Police and sheriff's deputies didn't spend much time patrolling out there. They would likely be responding from town. For now, Cole and his family plus Emma and Austin were on their own.

He heard raised voices inside the house. The bad guys were already inside. Cole couldn't tell how many thugs were in there, so he gestured at Emma to keep an eye on their surroundings in case one of the kidnappers had broken away from the group and snuck up behind them.

Cole eased the back door open, the loud voices apparently covering the squeaking sound. Then he moved forward down the hallway on the old wooden plank floor.

"Get out of our house!" Lauren shouted, followed by the sound of someone, presumably her, getting smacked.

"Shut up!" A different woman's voice. The female thug with the baby stroller who initiated the attack outside Super Mart.

"Please don't hurt us," Grandpa said in a broken, frail voice.

Cole smiled grimly. Grandpa was putting on a show. Trying to appear weak so he could take the criminals by surprise when he grabbed the gun he kept handy.

Cole took another couple of steps forward, trying not to let his attention get diverted by the threats one of the male

attackers was making toward Grandpa and Lauren in between demanding to know Emma and Cole's whereabouts.

One more step and Cole was able to peer into the front
room from the edge of the hallway. He saw Female Thug
and Bald Guy. Where were the other two kidnappers?
Where were Brent and Austin?

Grandpa sat in his favorite chair. The older man had one
of Lauren's knitted throws in his lap with his hands tucked
underneath it. The drawer in the table beside him had been
pulled out and it was empty. Very likely, Grandpa was
holding his handgun beneath that throw blanket. Faced
with multiple armed attackers, it was wise for the older
man to wait for the right moment to take action.

Cole's assumption was confirmed when Grandpa
caught sight of him hiding in the hallway. While continuing to cower and plead with Bald Guy not to hurt him and
his granddaughter, the older guy gave Cole a quick wink.

The female accomplice was on the other side of the
room, focused on keeping Lauren under control. Cole
still didn't see the other two kidnappers.

Emma made a soft sound before coming up behind
Cole so he wasn't startled. Turning slightly, he whispered,
"Stay here and run out the back door if things go side-
ways. *Please.*"

Emma nodded.

Cole's muscles tensed as he focused his gaze back on
Grandpa. The weathered old rancher looked him in the
eye and slowly raised his chin before suddenly dropping
it down. In that moment he pushed aside the throw blanket and revealed the pistol he'd hidden underneath. Cole
darted forward as Bald Guy and Grandpa fired at each
other at the same time, the sound deafening in the normally cozy room.

Fear that his grandfather had been shot energized Cole as he leapt onto Bald Guy's back, taking him by surprise and knocking him to the ground.

Female Thug fired a shot at Cole that missed him and struck a wall in the dining area. There was nothing Cole could do about her right now as he grappled on the floor with Bald Guy and furiously tried to wrest the gun from the criminal's grasp.

Bald Guy threw a hard punch that connected with Cole's jaw, shoving his face aside and forcing him to look in the direction of the Female Thug, who was now fighting back an attack from Lauren. Cole was grateful to see that his cousin could hold her own. His greater concern at the moment, however, was trying not to get shot by Bald Guy, who was still fighting with him. Cole gripped the wrist on the attacker's gun hand, twisting it to force the kidnapper to loosen his grip, but the criminal was strong and kept control of his weapon.

Finally Cole was able to shift his weight to an angle where he could jab his elbow into his assailant's midsection and knock the air out of the guy. Cole then gave another hard turn on the man's wrist and Bald Guy's grip loosened. Another twist and the gun finally dropped to the floor.

Grandpa was already on his feet and he kicked the weapon out of the Bald Guy's reach on his way to help Lauren as she still struggled with the armed woman.

Cole grabbed Bald Guy's shirt collar, pulled him partway up from the floor and then threw a jab that connected with the criminal's chin, knocking him out cold. He let the thug fall to the floor and then sprang to his feet, ready to help Lauren.

Lauren didn't need his help. Together, she and her

grandfather had disarmed the attacker she'd been fighting, and Female Thug was now face-down on the floor with her hands behind her back. Grandpa kept an eye on the criminal, his gun at the ready, while Lauren scrambled for a ball of yarn from a nearby basket to tie the woman's hands. When she was finished with that, she quickly moved to tie the bald assailant's hands before the creep regained consciousness.

Grandpa gave Cole a tired smile. "I think we got these two idiots under control."

Breathing hard after his fight, Cole nodded. "Yeah. But there are two more of them lurking around here somewhere." He grabbed the guns belonging to both attackers to make sure they couldn't recover them and then looked toward the hallway. "Emma!"

She darted into the room and grabbed him in a hug, her face buried in his shoulder.

"I'm all right," he said. "We're all okay."

"You won't be okay for long," the female criminal taunted with her face still pressed to the floor. "Our organization is big. Emma and her family know that only too well. You lock any of us up, they'll just send replacements. This is never going to end, Emma. Your family will never be safe."

"That's enough out of you," Grandpa growled.

The woman ignored him and kept talking. "Be a smart girl and work with us, Emma. Get your dad to shut up and refuse to testify at the trial. Get him to tell the court he made a mistake and identified the wrong man as the killer. Do that, and you'll see your little brother again."

"Austin!" Emma cried out in a horrified voice, pulling away from Cole. "Where's Austin?"

"Long gone by now," the assailant said with a harsh laugh. "Taken somewhere you'll never find him."

Emma's jaw went slack and tears immediately formed in her eyes.

"Ignore her," Cole said, letting disgust saturate his tone. In his overseas experience, combatants spoke all kinds of lies to try to dishearten and demoralize their opponents. He turned to his grandfather. "But we do need to find Austin. I know Brent was going to show him around and take him to the chicken coop to gather eggs. Do you know which way they went first?"

"Brent wanted to go to the chicken coop last so they could gather eggs and bring them directly to the house," Lauren interjected. "I think they were going the other direction to look at the goats, first."

Cole stepped over to a front window. Careful to move the curtain only slightly so as not to draw attention to himself, he took a look outside but didn't see anyone. He moved through the ranch house, looking out several other windows, but didn't see anyone and returned to the living room. "I don't know if Austin and Brent are nearby and just happen to be out of sight or if they're up at the stables or in the barn or somewhere else." *Or if they've been dragged away into the forest.*

While he was looking out the windows, Lauren had grabbed her phone and called 9-1-1. "Cops are almost here," she said to Cole with the phone up to her ear. "Maybe you should just wait inside."

"All of you should wait inside," Emma said in a steely tone, wiping the tears from her eyes. "But I *can't* wait. I've got to look for my brother. Maybe he's still on the property. I might be able to keep him from being taken away." She turned to Cole and held out her hand. "Give me your gun. I'm a decent shot," she added when he hesitated to respond. "My parents made me take a gun safety class and learn to shoot when we first moved here. I get out to the range every once in a while and practice with my dad's pistols. I know what I'm doing."

Cole handed over his gun, then grabbed the gun he'd taken away from Bald Guy and checked that it was loaded. "Let's slip out the door on the side of the house. It's possible the other two thugs haven't found Brent and your brother yet. We want to stay as quiet as we can and keep a low profile while we look around."

"Got it."

Cole nodded. "Let's go." He led the way to a small laundry room and looked out through a window in the door, but didn't see anyone. He took a breath and glanced at Emma before he slowly twisted the knob and took a cautious look outside.

"Emma Burke!" a voice called out from around the corner of the rambling house. "If you want to see your brother one last time, step outside now. Otherwise, you're never going to see him again."

Cole stilled. The voice sounded like it came from Ponytail Guy. He and the other assailant must have heard the shots fired inside the house. Since they hadn't heard from their partners, they could guess their fellow criminals had met with trouble. Beyond that, even if Emma hadn't been the one who'd opened the door, they knew their threatening message would be relayed to her.

Cole ducked back inside the house and turned to Emma. "Can you talk to them and distract them while I run through the house, go out another door and sneak up behind them?" he whispered.

She nodded. "Yes."

The mixture of fear and courage in her eyes touched his heart. Cole leaned forward, quickly pressed his lips against hers, then dashed into the house and headed for the door by the kitchen. It was possible that the two thugs outside had split up and he was walking into some kind of trap, but Emma had been right. They couldn't just wait inside the house for the cops to arrive. They had to do something to help Austin and Brent before it was too late.

Gun at the ready, Cole crept around the house, listening to the ongoing tense conversation between Emma and Ponytail Guy. Finally, he rounded a corner and found himself closely behind the guy who'd driven the getaway car outside of Super Mart. This creep was pointing a gun at Brent. Figuring there was no point in hesitation, Cole threw an arm across the criminal's neck and pressed hard against it, cutting off Getaway Guy's air supply while pressing his gun into the man's back. "Drop your weapon."

The attacker didn't comply at first, but then the pressure on his throat began to work and after fighting for breath, he finally dropped his gun. Cole kicked it away. Though there was no longer a gun pointed at him, Brent stood frozen to the spot, staring wide-eyed at Cole as if he were uncertain what to do.

Ponytail Guy, while still talking to Emma, kept his gun pointed at Austin. He took a quick glance at Cole. "Sent your boyfriend out here, huh, Emma?" He let go a barking laugh. "How about that. Here I was trying in good faith to negotiate with you, give you a chance to see your brother again, and this is what you do. You have your *sweetheart* sneak up on me."

"Let Austin go!" Emma yelled.

The criminal laughed harshly. "Not a chance. Grabbing him is what I get paid for. Come with us, Emma. You'll be fine. You and your brother can be together. We just don't want your dad to testify. That's it. The only thing it will take for your dad to save your lives is to shut up. How easy is that? And after the case falls apart and the trial is over, we'll let you and Austin go."

"Don't believe him, Emma!" Cole yelled. He knew under normal circumstances she'd be smart enough to see the lie. But her emotions had to be off the charts. And she'd been under so much stress the last few days.

"Listen to Cole," Austin added. "Ignore this creep."

Approaching sirens wailed in the distance. Ponytail Guy began backing up toward the tree line, dragging Austin with him. The criminals must have left a vehicle on the highway and hiked onto the property through the woods so they could sneak up on the house.

Cole was limited in what he could do. He was still holding on to Getaway Guy and needed to keep track of him. Brent, still standing there, would be an easy target if Ponytail Guy decided to take a shot at him to scare off any attempt at pursuit as the thug dragged Austin away. It felt like a stalemate where any action could get someone killed.

"Wait!" Emma called out.

Cole could hear the side door of the house slam behind her. She'd come outside.

"Let go of my brother!" Emma demanded. She held her gun, but it was pointed at the ground instead of at Ponytail Guy. The man was holding Austin as a shield, so if Emma tried to shoot him, she could accidentally hit her brother instead. She continued walking toward the retreating criminal.

Cole felt his heart rise up in his throat, terrified she was about to get shot.   •

Austin might have had the same fear as he suddenly twisted and attempted to fight off his captor. Afraid things were about to get deadly, Cole shoved Getaway Guy toward Brent, shouting, "Don't let him escape!"

Brent darted toward the criminal, receiving one hard slug to the jaw before knocking the criminal to the ground. Meanwhile, Cole raced toward Austin. Ponytail Guy was a much better fighter than Austin, and Emma's brother was getting pummeled. Before Cole could get to them, Emma leaped onto the back of the attacker fighting her brother.

Bang!

Cole reached the flurry of fighting and yelling just as a gun fired.

"Emma!" Cole grabbed for Ponytail Guy and the kidnapper collapsed under Cole's assault. Cole dropped down and pressed his knee against the man's back to keep him from getting away while also taking the man's gun. It was then that he realized the thug's leg was bleeding. He must have accidently shot himself.

Cole looked over at Emma as she squeezed her brother tightly. Austin appeared to hug her back with equal intensity.

"Everybody okay?" Cole called out, wanting to make certain no one else had been struck by a bullet.

"I'm fine," Emma replied.

"I'm all right, too," her brother said as the two of them finally stepped apart.

"Got everything under control here," Brent added.

Red-and-blue flashing lights appeared along the driveway coming through the forest. Police had finally arrived. Cole took a deep breath, trying to get his racing heart under control. The fights had been a challenge, but the fear that Emma had been hurt had nearly overwhelmed him.

Cole got to his feet beside the kidnapper. The man was crumpled in pain with a gunshot to his thigh, though the bleeding wasn't profuse. It didn't appear likely that Ponytail Guy could get away before the approaching cops took custody of him.

Cole turned to Emma and her gaze locked with his. She smiled tiredly, and then burst into tears. "Thank you," she said, laughing, though he didn't know why. Maybe she was laughing at the absurdity of the situation. Her reaction could also be the result of a sudden drop of adrenaline. Exhaustion was a likely possibility, too. As usual, Cole's paramedic brain wanted to figure out the cause of her upset and try to fix it.

"Thank you," Emma repeated, trudging toward him and then dropping a kiss on his lips like the one he'd given her a few minutes ago. Only this one lingered a bit longer.

"You don't need to thank me," Cole said. "You're the one who went after this guy—" he indicated Ponytail Guy "—and you brought an end to everything. I don't know how you did it."

"It's all that sugar I put in my coffee," she joked. "Gives me extra energy." Her smile softened. "Really, thank you for everything you've done for me. From the very start."

Cole looked into her eyes. Truth was he'd do pretty much anything she asked, anytime. There was no denying that now.

"Hey, you two trying to do my job?" Deputy Dylan Ruiz called out to them as he approached. His patrol car was parked nearby and three more cop cars were coming up the drive.

"Nope," Cole said. He nodded toward Emma. "*She's* the one who had to do your job for you."

Cole looked at Emma, thinking about his own job with

her at the fire department. About the two years they'd spent working together when he'd had no idea what an amazing, strong, compassionate woman she was. But that past was behind them. How would things be in the future? Would she and her brother be forced to change their identities again and go into hiding in some other town?

Right now, he didn't know. Just the thought of it made his heart feel hollowed out. He missed her already.

Storm clouds reached the ranch and began to pour down rain as the criminals were cuffed and put in separate patrol cars. There were plenty of law enforcement officers on scene now. It looked like half the cops in the county must have responded to the emergency call, including Cole's friends Deputy Dylan Ruiz and Officer Kris Volker.

To Emma's surprise, Sergeant Newman showed up, too.

"I thought you were assigned to the station on the other end of the county," she said when she found herself standing next to him on the front porch of the ranch house as they tried to get out of the rain. The inside of the house was packed with people and the temperature outside was refreshing after all the heated fighting and anxiety Emma had just been through. "How'd you get here to the ranch so quickly?"

"I happened to be at the main office in downtown Cedar Lodge working with some colleagues when the call came through," Newman told her. "Obviously, I was going to respond."

Made sense. He'd been in on this case since the original attack.

"Well, I guess now you know Austin didn't sell out our family." Emma couldn't keep the residual annoyance out of her voice. She glanced over at Austin, who was talking to Cole and Kris, and the two siblings shared a smile. The truth was she was grateful and relieved that things had turned out all right. The grudge she'd been holding against the witness protection task force member was something she needed to let go of. "Where did the idea that Austin had intentionally given away our family's location even start?"

Newman met her gaze. "It came from someone way above my paygrade who has access to your family's official records."

"Huh. Well, at some point I'd like to talk to that person about that. It was a dangerous idea to suggest. But they must have had some specific reason they thought it was a legitimate concern. I'd like to know what that was."

"How about we focus on something that will help wrap up your concerns over this entirely?" he suggested with an enigmatic smile. "Austin," he called out. "Could you come over and join us for a couple of minutes?"

Austin hustled in their direction. "What's up?"

"I want to let the both of you know that your concerns over your dad and the Royce Walker trial are at an end. Shortly before the initial call came out regarding the attack out here, Chief Ellis and I received notification that Royce Walker was shot and killed by rival gang members late this afternoon down in California. The trial is over before it even started, and I'm sure the criminal gang will leave you and your parents alone. They no longer have any reason to go after your dad or to try to kidnap you and your sister. They have a much bigger concern with the turf war that just got started. The dynamic of the gang will change.

You and your family will be the least of the new leadership's concerns."

Cole had drifted over by this point. He stood behind Emma and squeezed her shoulders lightly after Newman made his announcement.

Cole's nearness and his touch set her heart racing in ways it hadn't until a couple of days ago. How would things be as their lives went forward? How much had the kisses they'd exchanged meant something that could lead to a shared future, and how much of it was just due to the strong emotion of the moment?

The kisses meant something to her, but what about Cole? She'd misread his reactions before. If she had to go back to working alongside him as if nothing had changed between them, could she take it? Or would the daily reminder of how much she'd grown to care for him and how much his nearness to her affected her bring her too much heartache and grief?

"Hey, do our mom and dad know about this?" Austin asked Newman. He grabbed his phone from his pocket.

"Surely they would have called us." Emma reached for her phone, too. "Oh," she said immediately after unlocking the screen. "I've got some missed calls from both of them. And some texts."

"Me, too." Austin tapped his phone, as did Emma, to look to read the messages.

The next hour was a flurry of activity as Emma and Austin talked to their parents. Mom and Dad wanted Emma and Austin to come down to California so they could all be together and visit old friends. Austin was all for it, but Emma needed to get back to work. Both for the money and for the return to routine and normalcy that she'd been craving. Benny and Shawn were willing to come out to the ranch to get Austin and have him stay at their apartment until they took him to the airport tomorrow.

"Well, I suppose I should get going, too," Emma said to Cole an hour later after Austin left with his friends. All the cops were gone and everything seemed wrapped up for the moment. She'd been sitting at the dining table with the Webb family as they sipped hot chocolate, ate homemade banana bread and tried to wind down.

"Why don't you stay one more night?" Cole said. He sat beside her at the table, and while the rest of them had rehashed the day's events, he'd been fairly quiet. "It'll be raining hard on and off through the night." He gestured at a nearby window where rainwater splashed against the glass. "It's dark and sections of the road will likely be flooded. You're tired. How many calls have we gone on where someone rolled their vehicle or crashed because of that combination of conditions?"

"If you stay tonight, I'll make waffles in the morning," Lauren said with a tired smile.

Emma didn't actually want to leave. She liked staying there with the Webb family. Most especially, she'd liked spending so much time with Cole. She felt a tension between them, but this time *he* would have to be the one to bring up the topic.

But then again, maybe what she felt was *her* problem. It was possible that Cole had gotten as emotionally close to her as he cared to. The wise decision would be to get back to her apartment and her normal life as soon as possible. Get used to spending a lot of time alone again.

But she didn't want to be rude. "You know, I'll stay for more waffles," she said to Lauren, forcing a smile on her face.

Tomorrow Emma would make the break. Leave the ranch. And she and Cole would return to the professional relationship they maintained before all of this started.

FOURTEEN

"Shari just replied to my message and let me know they could use me at the library today," Emma told Cole the next morning before sliding her phone back into her pocket. The delicious breakfast Lauren had made was over, and now it was just Emma and Cole in the kitchen washing dishes again. "So add that to the chief agreeing to put me back on the EMT schedule and things have just about returned to normal."

"Good," Cole said, though he didn't feel at all good about her moving out. While the imminent danger over the last few days had been something he would never want to repeat, being around Emma virtually all day every day during that time was something he'd gotten used to. And he liked it. A lot. But how exactly did he tell her that? Especially when the vision he had for his future still wasn't clear.

Except when he'd tried to imagine his future, Emma showed clearly in it every time. Should he tell her that? Maybe it was too much and it would scare her off. Especially after she'd put her heart on the line trying to have an open, honest conversation with him and he'd balked like a stubborn mule.

Beyond that, what if they took a chance on developing

a relationship and it fell apart? What about their work relationship going forward?

Wanting to know things ahead of time, imagining scenarios and planning what he would do next, and considering all the variables was something he'd learned to do while in a war zone and had continued to do as a paramedic back home. But when it came to personal relationships and figuring out how he wanted things to go forward with Emma, that sort of thinking just wouldn't work. People and relationships weren't predictable.

He handed an oversized mixing bowl to Emma for her to dry, the last of the dishes that needed to be washed. Then he glanced at the old clock beside the refrigerator. "I've got to go. I'm going to be late for work."

"All right," Emma said without looking at him as she dried the bowl. "I'll be leaving soon, too. Thank you again for everything, and I'll see you later."

Was she mad at him? Or had she changed her mind regarding her feelings about him? Maybe all of this was just a case of over-the-top emotions coming to the surface during an intense situation.

"Emma..." He glanced at the clock again. He really had to get going. "I'll give you a call later today," he finally said, though he wanted to say a whole lot more. But this just wasn't the time.

"All right," she said brightly, her attention still on the bowl.

He walked out of the kitchen. Grandpa and Lauren and Brent were all outside taking care of their morning chores. Cole grabbed the daypack he usually brought to work with him and headed out the door.

The driveway was muddy after last night's rain, which made for slow going, but soon enough he was on the two-lane highway and headed toward downtown Cedar Lodge. After a few minutes of driving, a call came through from his grandpa. "What's up?" Cole asked over his truck's hands-free device.

"Do you know where Emma is?"

"Probably heading for work."

"Not without her vehicle."

Cole's blood chilled. "What are you talking about?" He slowed and looked for a place to pull off the road.

"Her SUV is still here, but she's nowhere to be found. I tried calling her a couple times because I was concerned, but she didn't answer. Just now Lauren and Brent went up to the stables and animal pens to have a look around in case she went over there."

Cole had found a spot where he was able to turn. "I'm on my way back. Call me if you hear from her. I'll be there in a few minutes."

He floored it back to the ranch and up the muddy drive to the house, hoping that he'd see Emma standing on the porch and find out that Grandpa's concern had all been a misunderstanding. But that wasn't the case. Instead, Grandpa and Lauren and Brent were all standing on the wide porch, looking worried.

"Do you think we should call 9-1-1?" Lauren asked as he got out of the truck and ran up the steps.

"I think you'd better," Cole replied, hurrying past her and into the ranch house to get his gun. He'd thought danger had passed and so he'd stopped carrying it. "Let's take a look around and see what kind of tracks we can find," he said as he returned to the living room where his family were all waiting and Lauren was on the phone with an emergency operator.

"I'm going to head in the direction the attackers came

from yesterday," Cole said. "Kris told me the cops found the kidnappers' car on that old logging road. They'd left it there and hiked in. If somebody's taken Emma, they might have tried doing the same thing.

"I'm going to take a horse," Cole added as he tucked his gun beneath his waistband. "I don't want to take an ATV and risk giving away my location if I'm coming up on a thug who might have grabbed Emma."

He strode out to the porch and the others followed him.

"How can we help?" Lauren asked.

The last thing Cole wanted to do was put his family in danger. They were good at surviving in the wilderness and at tracking, but none of them had been trained for a criminal encounter or combat. Last night's battle when they fought off the criminals was their first, and he hoped last, experience with that.

"You should probably arm yourselves," he said.

Grandpa pulled aside the front of his corduroy jacket so Cole could see the pistol at his waist. Cole nodded. "Good. You all stay here at the house."

"I'm not going to do that," his grandfather said.

Cole wasn't surprised. "Look, I can check the perimeter faster than any of you. As soon as I find relevant tracks, I'll let you know. If you stay here and I have to call for help, you could all gather together faster if you're in the house than if you're spread out all over the property." He took a steadying breath and blew it out. "And if Emma's just been out hiking around on the property outside of cell range and she comes back to the house, you can let me know right away."

Without waiting for their response, Cole ran to the stables. He saddled up his favorite mare, Suzie, as quickly as he could and then rode off. The edge of the drive looked like the best place to start and from there he rode along the tree line where forest met the grassy clearing surrounding the house. He set a moderate pace where he could cover a reasonable amount of ground while at the same time looking for broken twigs or branches or footsteps or recently disturbed mounds of pine needles on the forest floor.

His muscles tensed with stress as his focus narrowed on searching for signs of which way Emma might have gone. He trotted along for a hundred yards or so before he spotted a freshly snapped twig and reined in Suzie to a stop. She snorted impatiently, obviously warmed up and ready for a good gallop. Cole dismounted, patted his horse on the neck to hopefully quiet her a little, and then took several steps into the forest. The freshly disturbed ground confirmed someone had come this way very recently. Looked like it was at least two people.

After taking several more steps, holding onto the reins so Suzie didn't wander off, an uneasy mixture of dread and relief settled in his stomach. There, caught in a bundle of thick green pine needles, were several strands of sable-colored hair, just the color of Emma's. It was good to know which way she'd gone. It was terrifying to know some criminal must have finally gotten hold of her. For what reason someone would take her at this point, he had no idea. Didn't matter. He had to find her.

Cole placed a quick call to his grandfather to let him know what he'd found and where. "Let the cops know," he said before disconnecting. Then he stepped onto a stirrup and swung up into the saddle on Suzie's back. He drew his gun before giving the horse a gentle kick to get her moving. All the while he kept an eye out in case he was being watched.

* * *

Once again Emma had a gun pointed at her head, only this time it was held by a cop.

"Keep moving," Sergeant Newman growled after Emma caught her toe on an exposed tree root and had to flail her arms to keep her balance.

Emma's heart had pounded in fear the moment the sheriff's deputy grabbed her as she'd gone out to get into her SUV, and it hadn't stopped racing since.

The deputy was dressed in a coat with the hood pulled down and the collar flipped up, presumably so he'd be unidentifiable if anyone saw him from a distance. But Emma had recognized his voice when he'd approached her from behind, and none of the things that had happened afterward made any sense.

"Where are we going?" she asked for the third or fourth time.

As before, he didn't answer. He just shoved her and forced her to keep moving faster.

"*Why* are you doing this?"

"Don't tell me you haven't figured it out by now."

"What are you talking about?" she shot back. It probably would have been smarter to keep her tone placating so he wouldn't get mad and shoot her on the spot, but she was at the point where her fear was turning to anger.

"You asked me last night why I focused the blame on Austin for your family's location being disclosed and where that information came from. You said you were going to start an investigation into that."

"Yeah, so?" Her mind raced over what he'd just told her. Why would any of that matter? Did he think he'd get in trouble for blaming the wrong person? But it was somebody else with witness protection who'd come up with the idea that Austin was responsible. Why would Newman get the blame?

He'd been lying when he said that. An idea formed in her mind that seemed unbelievable, and yet it fit. Fit the situation right now. Fit with everything. "Did *you* give the Walker gang my family's location?"

He didn't answer. She wanted him to. She wanted him talking because if anyone was looking for them maybe they'd hear his voice. Or hear her voice if she kept talking. Then again, maybe no one was looking for her. Maybe none of the Webb family had gone back to the house yet and they didn't realize her car was there but she was missing. Maybe she was on her own.

No, not on her own. *Lord, please help me. Please be with me and guide me.*

"Did you sell them the information about us?" she pressed.

"See, I knew you'd figure it out."

"But I hadn't."

"Well, now you know for sure and you won't be able to do anything about it."

She didn't know for certain what that meant, but she had a pretty good idea. And if he planned to execute her out here in the woods, she wasn't going to make it easy for him.

They reached a creek, swollen with water from the recent rains and natural dams created by deposits of forest debris. Emma paused at the edge, looking in both directions and desperately trying to see how she could escape or where she could hide. Newman pushed her and her feet sank into the mixture of mud and pine needles. He pushed her again and this time she fell, landing in the cold, briskly moving water and unavoidably taking in a mouthful. She pushed herself partway up, coughing and spitting out the water and trying to catch her breath.

Sirens sounded in the distance.

Newman crossed the creek and turned to face her. "This is as good a place as any to do this." He pulled out a second gun from beneath his jacket and pointed it at her.

"What are you doing?!" Panic clawed at Emma's chest.

"I got this pistol off one of the idiots who got himself captured last night," Newman said, gesturing with the second gun. "I'm going to shoot you. The cops will find the round inside your body and possibly the gun if I drop it nearby. Hopefully the police will then connect all the evidence I'm leaving behind to the Walker gang. Detectives will focus their murder investigation on those lowlifes and I'll be off the hook."

Murder investigation. He meant to kill her right here, right now.

Figuring at this point she had nothing to lose, Emma pushed off her hands and knees and scrambled up the creek bank. Running as fast as she could, she heard a gunshot fired in her direction. It was followed by another, and before she got very far she was compelled to dive to the ground behind a large tree so she didn't get hit. Seconds later she heard more gunshots, only these came from a different direction and they didn't sound like they were aimed at her. They were accompanied by the sounds of breaking tree branches and unnaturally heavy footsteps.

Emma peered around the tree and saw Cole. He was on horseback, with his gun pointed toward Newman. "Drop your weapon!"

The disgraced deputy, who had both his hands held up, let the pistol he was still holding drop to the ground.

"Emma?" Cole called out.

"I'm here!" She stepped out from behind the tree. On shaky legs, she headed toward Cole as he dismounted his horse.

Cole moved forward. Emma headed in his direction, and as she got closer to Newman she saw the deputy make a sudden move. In a flash, she realized he'd reached for his other gun, and without questioning her decision Emma flung herself at him.

Newman staggered under the weight of her surprise attack, giving Cole enough time to rush toward him and throw a flurry of hard punches that quickly had the criminal cop off-balance and ultimately knocked unconscious. Newman dropped to the ground.

Cole quickly secured the deputy's guns as Emma got to her feet.

"You found me!" Emma said breathlessly. Exhausted by physical strain and the aftereffects of so much fear coursing through her body, she staggered toward Cole and he swept her up in his arms. Pressed up against him, she could feel his heart pounding in his chest.

"Of course I found you," he said. "I wouldn't have stopped looking until I did."

It was all too much, and Emma burst into tears. Cole hugged her even tighter. At some point she would have to let him go. She knew that. But she also knew that she wasn't ready to do that yet.

FIFTEEN

Two hours later Sergeant Newman had been arrested and taken away and all the necessary police statements had been given.

Emma had showered and changed into clothes not covered with mud and creek water and forest floor debris. Now she stood in the doorway of her room at the Webb family ranch, making sure she hadn't left anything behind. "It's over," she said to herself softly.

She was thinking of the threats to her family as well as herself. Of course, she'd thought it was over once before, after the four thugs had been arrested. Then Sergeant Newman had shown up out of the blue to kidnap her with the intention of murdering her and hiding her body in the forest.

But she had survived. *Thank You, Lord.* In some regard there were always risks and potential dangers in life. Emma wasn't flippant about that realization. Her nerves were still stretched tight after the attack in the forest. Her hands still trembled a little. Her mind wanted to snap her back to some of the most frightening moments and push her to relive them again. But she knew that it was all part of processing trauma. Something she'd first become aware of eight years ago after her dad witnessed Royce Walker committing murder and the whole family had their lives changed.

Emma's stay with the Webb family was at an end. She would miss waking up at the ranch in the morning with its surrounding forest and gorgeous view of the nearby jagged mountain peaks. She'd miss the warm hospitality of Cole's grandpa and Lauren and Brent. She'd miss the animals, especially the dogs, Liza and Misty, and the good, strong coffee that was always available and the substantial made-from-scratch breakfasts.

Most of all, she would miss Cole and the closeness they'd shared.

Thank You, Lord, she prayed again, trying to focus on gratitude for what she had experienced with getting to know Cole rather than the heartache she felt now that it had all come to an end. It might be difficult to work alongside him in the future knowing that he didn't love her the way she loved him, but she would get used to it.

What she felt truly was *love*, after all. She knew that now. It wasn't just a desire to somehow possess him because he was handsome and courageous and compassionate. She genuinely wanted the best for him. Whatever made him happy. Whatever gave him peace. And if that meant forcing herself to take a step back from him emotionally, she would do exactly that. Or at least give the appearance that she had. For his sake.

She turned from the bedroom, packed bag in hand, and headed out to the living room.

Emma had said her goodbyes to everyone before she'd gone to her room to pack up. Grandpa, Lauren and Brent all had work to do around the ranch this morning and Sergeant Newman's kidnapping of Emma had already gotten in the way of them accomplishing their tasks.

Cole had been scheduled for a twelve-hour shift before he'd been forced to turn around and return to the ranch after learning that Emma was missing. He could still get in at least eight hours on the ambulance, and Emma didn't want to be responsible for him losing any more work hours and income. Besides that, a quick parting of ways was easier on her and undoubtedly more convenient for Cole.

She was surprised, then, to see him when she walked into the living room.

"Hey," he called out. He looked nervous, which was unusual for him. He shoved his hands into his jeans pockets and leaned back on his heels.

"Hey, yourself," Emma said cautiously. She set down her bag.

"I made some coffee," he added after a moment. There were two mugs on the table close to him. He picked up one and handed it to her.

Emma glanced down at the contents. The brew looked more like hot chocolate. She took a sip. It was chocolaty and very sweet, just as she liked it. "Thanks," she said cautiously. Was he buttering her up for some reason? Did he want something from her? All he had to do was ask. She owed him big-time and she knew it.

The way he looked at her started to make her feel jittery and nervous. But not in a bad way. In a way that drew her in, almost physically, as she found herself wanting to move closer to him. Her heartbeat sped up a little, compelling her to find out exactly what was on his mind. "Don't you need to get to work?" she asked, before taking another sip of the mocha coffee.

She offered him an encouraging smile, and the expression on his face slowly changed. He stopped fidgeting. He squared his shoulders and solidified his stance, and now he looked like the confident man she'd always known him to be. The calm and collected paramedic. The self-assured military veteran.

"What I need is to have you by my side." A soft smile crept across his lips.

Now Emma was the nervous one. She thought she might know where this was going. But she was afraid she might be wrong. "You'll have me by your side soon enough. You know I'm already back on the work schedule."

"That's not what I mean." Cole reached for her coffee mug and slid it from her fingers. He set it on the table, and then reached for her hands. "I had no idea what I was missing out on, but now I do."

She blinked at him, still afraid to get her hopes up.

"I thought my life would be better if I played it safe," Cole said. "Well, my *personal* life, I should say. I thought it would be wiser not to take too much of a risk in trusting a person. I was afraid to truly fall in love with a woman because what if things didn't turn out the way I hoped? What if it was a mistake?"

"I don't know how many guarantees there are in life, really," Emma said quietly. "Every day is a blessing, and we forget that sometimes. I know I did. But I've sure been reminded of that lately."

"Me, too." He stepped forward, took her in his arms and kissed her.

All Emma could do was blink after the warm, lingering kiss was over. The combination of happiness and security she felt had her wanting to simply soak up the moment. Cole had talked about the risk of expecting something in a relationship and potentially not getting it. Well, Cole Webb had turned out to be something she *hadn't* expected. And she was a little bit afraid of the hope building in her heart, because right now it felt out of control and impossible to restrain.

Cole wasn't the only one who was nervous.

"I know you, Emma," Cole said. "I've spent time with you, I've seen you take action and express concern and caring. You're smart and funny and you make me laugh."

"This is quite a change from just a couple of nights ago," she said gently. The last thing she wanted to do was derail where this conversation was going. But she wanted their relationships to be solid, so she needed to understand. "What changed your mind?"

"Thinking about it. Knowing you were worth the risk. Realizing that whenever I pictured myself with a happy future, you were there."

Emma laughed. She couldn't help it. His analytical paramedic's brain doing a risk assessment on falling in love with her was so spot on for him. But it was all right, because these last few days had proven to her that behind his practical nature Cole Webb did have a very warm and loving heart.

"Just so you know, I'm taking a risk with you, too," she teased.

"I know." Cole wrapped his arms around the small of her back and pulled her closer. "What do you say we take a chance and do our best to work things out together?"

"After all we've been through, I'm pretty sure we already know we can do that."

Cole leaned in for another kiss, this one lingering even longer than the first. Emma's knees went weak, but it wasn't from nerves; it was from sheer joy. By the time the kiss was over and Cole began nuzzling the side of her neck, she was actually beginning to feel lightheaded. Good thing she had a paramedic on hand.

One year later

Cole swept Emma up in his arms and carried her over the threshold and into the front room at the Webb family ranch house.

"Welcome home!" Lauren and Brent called out in unison.

Austin and Grandpa, both smiling mischievously, each brought a hand from behind their backs and flung bright confetti at the newlyweds, who'd just returned from their honeymoon in the Bahamas.

"About time you two got back," Grandpa said in a mock-complaining tone. "There's work to be done around here."

"That's right!" Austin teased in a tone that sounded remarkably like the older man. "You've been goofing off long enough!"

Laughing and smiling, Emma reached up to brush the confetti from her hair. Austin and Grandpa had hit it off and spent a lot of time working together at the ranch over the last year. Austin, especially, had benefited from the friendship and had become much more confident as he'd learned new skills and developed the beginnings of a real rancher's work ethic.

Cole still hadn't put Emma down. She turned to him and he planted a quick kiss on her lips, followed by several more, until he finally set her on her feet. "Welcome home," he said.

Home.

It hadn't taken long for Emma and Cole to decide they wanted to get married. The wedding had taken place at the church Emma's family had been attending since they'd moved to Cedar Lodge, and her mom and dad had insisted on paying for the reception at Elk Ridge Resort. They'd had a nice dinner in the resort's steakhouse located near the edge of a mountain ridge with a beautiful view of the lights of the town of Cedar Lodge sparkling down below.

Grandpa had told them he'd be delighted if they lived at the ranch. Making it their home was an easy decision. Emma loved being there, and she and Cole both thought it would be a great place to raise children.

"I'll go get our bags," Cole said, before planting a kiss on Emma's cheek and then going back out for their luggage.

"Lauren and Brent are teaching me how to make a cherry pie from scratch," Austin told his sister with a wide grin. He walked over to give her a hug. "We should probably get back at it if we want to have the pie for dessert tonight." Lauren and Brent each gave Emma a welcome-home hug before the baking trio wandered off to the kitchen.

Grandpa gave her a hug as well, and then headed for the dining room table with a crossword puzzle book and a couple of mechanical pencils in his hand.

The household was settling into their early-evening routines and that was just how Emma loved it. Life was back to normal in some ways and completely different in others. Emma and Cole both continued to work for the Cedar Lodge Fire Department, but the chief made certain they were assigned to different crews, which seemed to Cole and Emma like a wise idea.

Cole came back into the house with their luggage, took it to their bedroom, then returned to embrace Emma in yet another hug. He never seemed to get tired of wrapping his arms around her, and Emma had no complaints about that.

"Those years we worked together I had no idea you were so cuddly," she said, smiling.

"It took the right woman to bring out the best in me," Cole said, hugging her again.

"And the right man to bring out the best in me," Emma said into his shoulder.

Both of them had needed the love and support of someone else to learn how to face life's challenges with grace and acceptance and forgiveness. They'd also needed faith strong enough to push through the tough times. Faith had brought them this far, and ultimately faith would bring them all the way home.

* * * * *

If you enjoyed this
Big Sky First Responders
book by Jenna Night, be sure
to pick up the first in the series,
Deadly Ranch Hideout,
available now from Love Inspired!

Dear Reader,

It's such a good feeling when we are pleasantly surprised by someone. A coworker who lends a hand when we're running behind on a task at work. A neighbor who does something thoughtful. An acquaintance who ultimately becomes a dear friend.

I love stories where people have a relationship that's been going along the same way for a while and then one day things are different. Maybe one of the people has somehow changed. Or maybe the only thing that's changed is one person's *perception* of the other. Either way, these types of stories are fun. Emma and Cole's situation is a version of that, and I hope you enjoyed reading about them.

The Big Sky First Responders series has more danger and opportunities for falling in love coming your way soon! Please sign up for my newsletter at jennanight.com to stay up-to-date. You can also find the most recent book release information by following me on BookBub or Facebook or Goodreads. And if you're so inclined, feel free to drop me a line at Jenna@JennaNight.com.

See you next time!
Jenna Night